Tales from the Basement

Tales from the Basement

Hastings College Press | *Hastings, Nebraska*

© 2024 Hastings College Press

All rights reserved. No part of this book may be used or reproduced in any manner whatsoever without permission from the publisher, except in the case of brief quotations embodied in critical articles and reviews.

ISBN: 978-1-942885-94-8

Contents

How can I adequately explain the deep unease I feel in describing for you the tales in this volume? Gathered through both personal experience and hushed conversations with those who wish to forget, these stories are the result of a late-morning contest of terror. In the dreary days of September 2024, twenty-two devotees of dread gathered around a faux fireplace in the basement of the Wilson Mathematics and Computer Science Building to share true-life stories of ghosts and the gothic. Oh, would that some science, whether normal or paranormal, could expel the terror of these tales! But alas, a chill—due to the frightening performances of the readers or the overactive air conditioning, no one knows—permeated the hearts of all who listened. I present these tales to you now, readers, as I heard them on that morning. I cannot tell you that the events herein described are real, but the tellers assure me of their truth. Of course that is what they would say when their grade depends on it.

—P. Oman

HAMZA ABBASI

On a cold and chilly December night, when fog from the river Thames had settled over the colossal grounds outside, covering them as if nature had put a large white sheet on them, Jamal ran over to the library, as he was already late for his shift on his first day of work. His shift was supposed to start at midnight, but it was already an hour past that. Jamal had recently landed a job in one of the oldest and most prestigious libraries in the country. It was situated in a very remote part of the countryside. He was supposed to work there as a janitor three times a week. Any three days of his choosing. His employer Mrs. Armada was a gentle and sweet old soul, but Jamal didn't want to get on her bad side on his first day. Jamal had previously encountered trouble keeping a job, as he was having a hard time dealing with PTSD from the Great War because of the choices he made and the things he had done. He was starting to struggle a bit too as the economy after the war had crashed, in 1920, so he really needed this job to stick. So here he was, away from friends and family, all alone in the remote countryside trying to make a job stick.

After the horrors Jamal had witnessed during the war nothing scared or phased him much anymore, but as he rushed over to the library his mind kept racing to the rumors he had heard from his friends. The library, nay the whole building, was haunted, but Jamal didn't believe in ghosts. Just overactive imaginations and exaggerated events. Jamal, for one, had never set foot in a library before, let alone this one, so he kept trying to brush the thoughts about the hauntings aside. The building itself was constructed like a medieval castle with high rising towers and arches, the whole deal. Considering how old it was, it could probably have been a castle at some point in time. As soon as he swung open the library door a flash of lightning lit up the library with a thunderous roar soon followed by heavy downpour. Jamal's agnostic mind swept it away as a simple coincidence. Jamal didn't believe in omens, unlike his great-grandmother, who used to be a psychic seer. In fact, Jamal came from a whole line of psychics from his mother's side. Jamal on the contrary liked to base his world view on solid and objective fact. The library was empty because not only was it past midnight but not many visited it in the first place due to its remote location. The library was kept open, nevertheless, by the government because of its significance as a historic site.

While Jamal was sweeping in the oldest corner of the library, he saw a portrait: a tall man with good posture, in a military uniform. What particularly stood out to Jamal were the four pentagrams engraved in the four corners of the frame. He had heard his mother say that occultists often did that to create a "portal" of sorts between the plane of the living and the dead. A plaque at the bottom read "Colonel Azarath Zintos." Jamal tried to look up information on the colonel in the library but couldn't find much. It turned out that the building, in fact, used to be a castle. The colonel used to live there and had been a cruel baron who got overthrown and killed by his subjects in a previous age. Jamal wasn't too surprised considering his own experience with his CO during the war.

After Jamal was done cleaning half the library, exactly at 3:30 am, he felt a cold shiver run down his spine. It was as if someone had traced a cold bony finger down it. Jamal once again didn't think much of it until he heard a low soft whisper, almost like a grunt: "Return the book." Jamal froze. "Who's there?" he asked, as his voice trembled. At this point in time his palms were sweaty, knees weak, arms were heavy. He was nervous, but on the surface he looked calm and ready. "RETURN THE BOOK," pounded his ears once more like a loud bang, shattering all the windows in the library at once. The rain and shards of glass came crashing down on the library floor. Jamal fell down on his back trembling with fear and just then a transparent figure dressed in an old-fashioned military uniform appeared. Jamal instantly recognized the apparition. It was the exact same person from the portrait he had seen earlier.

The colonel repeated once again, "Return the book." Jamal replied nervously, "What book?" The colonel floated closer until he was an inch away from his face. Jamal, who could see right through the colonel's cold, lifeless eyes, heard, "The one you borrowed in 1831." Jamal looked straight into the ghost's eyes and said, "Oi! You mad bruv? That's what up innit? I wasn't even born then. Me great granny was just a wee baby." The colonel looked confused for a while and then said, "Oh, sorry. Wrong guy." The baron then disappeared leaving behind the cold rain and a very relieved janitor. Jamal laughed at the encounter and said to himself, "At least it wasn't overdue fines! That would have been bonkers."

The Wheat Growers Window

SHANNEN ACHESON

They say that history repeats itself, and sadly this is often true. The Wheat Growers Hotel may have once been a grand attraction, but now it is nothing more than a trap filled with tortured souls. I don't remember much of how this became the extent of my world, but I have seen it repeat enough on other people to be able to piece it together. I wish I knew why this became my fate. Was this always meant to be my ending?

Asking questions is pointless, so instead I spend my time wandering through the halls aimlessly. There is nothing else for me to do. Mice scamper from my path, hiding in dark corners and crevices. I am not certain if they can see me or if they turn and flee simply because they sense my presence. Perhaps it is not my presence they fear but that of the wailing woman who busies herself by staring out the corner window on the third floor.

I do not know her name. I do not know her truth. I only know the story that everyone believes, the story of a young woman working in a speakeasy. Despite dwelling in the same rundown hotel as her, I am at a serious loss when it comes to information. You would think that her being the reason I died might entitle me to some conversations with her, but alas. She is so far gone I sometimes wonder if she even knows she killed me.

She fascinated me before I died, even more so now. For decades, people in Kimball have told stories of the Wheat Growers Hotel. It is said that a young woman died when a hidden tunnel collapsed on her. No one ever mentions how or why the tunnel collapsed or any-thing too detailed about who she was. She is described as only a nameless, faceless ghost who is forever tied to the abandoned hotel.

Despite the lack of information regarding the woman, the stories are partially correct. Her ghost is tied to the hotel. I have tried to follow her around the hotel on the rare occasions she leaves the third-floor window, but every time we make it to the marble stairs leading to the basement she simply flickers and disappears. She returns to the window, sometimes hours or days later.

The sound of a door creaking open piques my interest enough to change course from my regular route. Instead of walking straight down each separate hall as I normally do, I zigzag through crumbled walls and down the stairs to the first floor. The back door has been opened, letting the moonlight and the crisp autumn air into the dusty building. I spot two teenagers, a boy and a girl, standing just inside the back entrance and my heart sinks to my stomach, or whatever the ghost equivalent is.

This is the beginning of my story, just as it is the beginning of several other ghosts' stories here. The others have long since given up, but I still try to save the young souls who dare to enter the Wheat Growers in search of the wailing woman's truth.

The teenagers tiptoe down the hall, probably looking for the basement. I have not yet mastered the ability to be seen by the living, so I instead focus on moving objects around them. I know that the closer they get to the basement the less likely they are to leave.

Just as I go to slam a door, I see the wailing woman rushing towards the teenagers. They shiver as she passes through them, and I see a shift in the boy's eyes. I watch helplessly as he grabs the girl's arm.

"Sam, that hurts! Stop it!" The girl twists her arm in an attempt to escape his grip. Her eyes widen in fear as he yanks her toward the stairs. I move in front of them assuming they are still going to the basement. He instead drags her behind as he moves up the stairs to the first floor.

I follow as quickly as I can, but the wailing woman is pushing me back. She has been here the longest of all of us, and she is stronger than me. If I were still alive, I would describe it as an out-of-body experience. Sleep paralysis might be more accurate. This is a nightmare I am all too familiar with.

The cause of death is never the same. The wailing woman is creative. I wish I could tell you what my death was like, but I have no memory. I do remember the boy who banged his head against the wall until he couldn't anymore and the girl who impaled herself on the broken support beam on the second floor. I remember all the deaths because I witnessed them just as I am about to witness two more, but no one was here for me. Only the wailing woman.

My thoughts begin to swirl and blend as I watch the pair continue to the third floor, unknowingly following the wailing woman. I can do nothing to stop it as the boy—Sam, she called him—climbs out onto the fire escape. The wailing woman guides their path onto the roof, and I feel compelled to follow as well.

The girl is hysterical, crying and screaming for help, but it is no use. No one is coming to save her. Tears stain her face as she whispers to the boy. "I love you. Please stop. Please." Her voice cracks with emotion.

I am waiting for him to push the girl from the roof, but that moment never comes. Instead, he grabs a rope that is lying on the ground and wraps it around the girl's neck. I see it before it happens. All it takes is a minute and he is holding the rope while she dangles lifeless at the side of the building.

The momentum of her fall should be enough to pull him over as well, but he does not budge. He stands upright as if he is holding a feather or nothing at all.

He releases the rope, and I hear the sickening crack as her body meets the sidewalk below. He takes several steps forward until his toes are over the edge. He turns to the wailing woman with a smile and leans forward. Murder-suicide. How creative.

The boy meets the ground with the same stomach-curdling crunch. Their bodies line up with their hands overlapping, almost intertwined. One final, sick twist of fate. That is the last thing I remember from their death. The thoughts and emotions fighting inside me suddenly go quiet. Too suddenly.

I lose awareness. I do not know how long I have been drifting. Blurry images of the boy and the girl, their death, and the stairs twist around in my mind, toying with my consciousness. When I awake I have a beautiful view of the street and the railroad tracks. The same view the wailing woman has from her corner window on the third floor.

Waiting for No One

ANN BOSE

My name is Judy, and my husband's name is Kyle. We live outside a small town on a farm in a big, beautiful, white house. My days consist of the same routine over and over. I can't complain. I get to stay at home with our dog, Ace, all day. Ace loves me, but I'm more of a "spare human" for him. He loves Kyle much more, and if he had a choice, he would choose him over me any day. I cook, I clean, I take Ace for walks, I read, cook again and repeat. Kyle wakes up way earlier than I do and comes home long after I'm asleep. He's a farmer, so there are things to be done, bills to be paid. I love the life we are building, but let me tell you a story about the strangest day of my life.

It was a normal Wednesday about a month ago. I started my day the same as always. I woke up, let Ace outside, and started breakfast. I started scrambling the eggs when I realized we were out of milk, so I turned off the stove and loaded Ace up to head into town and get a couple groceries. Ace always gets super excited for car rides because he thinks we're going to see his dad, but we haven't got to do that in quite some time. When I got back to the house, I noticed the stove was still on and the eggs were scrambled but on the verge of being burnt. I rushed over and took the pan off the stove. It was weird because I could've sworn I turned the stove off, but I ignored this and went on with my day. I showered, cleaned the kitchen, and took Ace for a walk. I then sat down in the living room in my chair, right next to my husband's Lazy Boy.

I have never got to experience us together in this room in our chairs, just being a normal couple, but I don't complain. I cracked open my book and began to read. This is when the footstool on my husband's chair popped out and the back reclined as if someone had just got in it. Ace was laying in front of me on the rug, and he didn't even flinch. If Ace didn't care, then I wasn't about to care, so I went about my reading. After reading one too many chapters I decided it was time to make some supper. I decided to make Kyle's favorite meal so that he could eat leftovers when he got home. He loves tater tot casserole because his mom used to make it for him as a kid, so I try to make it as often as I can to make him happy. After I finished eating and cleaning, I started toward my bedroom when I remembered I had forgot to put the leftovers in the fridge. When I got to the kitchen, the leftovers weren't on the counter but in the fridge. Guess I didn't forget.

When I reached my bedroom, I threw on my pajamas and got into bed. I try to stay up later to see Kyle when he gets home, but I normally can't. Tonight I decided to read to pass time, but I eventually gave up and clicked off the lamp. I lay in bed for what felt like hours without being able to fall asleep. That is when it happened. I heard the door open and got so happy. My husband slipped right into bed with me and for the first time in a long time I felt him under the covers with me, but it didn't last long. He soon got up and left the room. I turned the lamp back on and called him. His dad answered. I asked him if he knew where Kyle was....

"Wait, wait, wait, you said you *felt* Kyle under the covers with you?" said Amanda, my mom.

"Yes, it was my favorite part of the day," I said.

"Baby, Kyle has been dead for over a year now. I told you I think you need to come live with me. I'm worried about you."

"No!" I yelled. "I have to wait for Kyle to come home."

Daisies of Mourning

BROOKE BROCKMAN

I thought this was the end. Here I am outside of the house my husband bought a few months ago, scared to go in because of a, well, you wouldn't believe it if I told you. Well, I have nothing else planned for a few hours. How about I tell you what happened? It started a few months ago. I just got back from, let's say, overseas. The car was playing "Dreams" by Fleetwood Mac. He used to love that song, just like … My thoughts get interrupted by a loud honk. Okay, I'm going, geeze. I had just gotten to this beautiful, brick two-story house. It had an apple tree in the front yard with daisies. I smiled at the scene. He really knows how to pick a house, I thought. A single tear fell down my face. The door suddenly opened. I grabbed a fallen apple and threw it at the shadowy creature.

"Ow!" the voice said. The shadow came out to the light. "Sorry. I guess I should have called," Clara said. I just rolled my eyes.

"You're lucky I didn't pull out my gun," I signed. She laughed. She waved me over to come in. I followed her and shut the door. She quietly showed me around the house. It was pretty simple: big living room, two bedrooms, attic, and the basement. When we went back to the living room, she looked at me and looked down at the giant scar on my neck. She put her hand on my shoulder and gave it a squeeze.

"How are you really doing?" she asked. I sighed.

"I thought it was the end," I signed. *"How do I keep going on after everything that happened?"* Clara looked at me and gave me a hug.

"If you would be more comfortable, I can stay the night, if you want?" I wiped my eyes and shook my head.

"No, I'll be fine." I opened the door. *"Do you mind leaving?"* Clara passed me and told me goodbye. The door shut softly. I wrapped myself in a blanket and sat on the rocking chair. Slowly I went to sleep.

I hate mornings, especially when I have job interviews. Yeah right, like I would get any. But we have to remain positive. It's what he would have wanted, right? I put my thoughts aside and got in my car. "Take on me" by A-HA started to play. I was doing little dances while I was driving.

"*I went to five interviews, Clara. Guess what they all said to me?*" I signed to her.

"I don't know," Clara said. "It's hard to dictate tone with signs," she said sarcastically.

"*Can you read this sign?*" I signed and then flipped her off. She laughed.

"*They said we don't have any jobs that would work with your abilities.*" Clara dropped her string stick in shock. "*That's not all. They also told me thank you for your service.*"

Clara slowly drank her coffee. "You know that's against the Disability Act, right?" I nodded. "We can sue the pants off these companies and you won't even have to worry about money right now."

I looked at her softly and grabbed her hands. "*I don't need that right now,*" I signed. "*And I don't need help from your lawyer friends.*"

"Why won't you let me help you?" she asked.

"*Don't you have anyone else to bug?*" I signed. She shook her head. "*For people like me it won't work out that way.*"

Clara looked at me and smiled. "But you'll find your own special way to make it work."

I then paid for our coffee and left.

Back at home I decided to go through some stuff and take it to the basement. You know, basic stuff like holiday decorations, coats, and uniforms. I slowly walked down the stairs. There was a creak with each step. I got to the bottom of the stairs and the door slammed shut. My breathing started to quicken. I put the boxes in the farthest corner of the room and began to hug myself. Calm down! It's just a loose door. You are home. YOU ARE HOME! I looked up and the door was open. I rubbed my eyes and looked upstairs again. The door was still open. I blinked a few times and then got up, grabbed the boxes, and put them on the shelves. I quietly walked up the stairs and thought to myself, I have to get my episodes under control.

I avoided the basement like the plague after that incident. I got everything else unpacked. I smiled at all the work I did. I got on the couch and wrapped myself in a blanket and put on some TV. Then there's this scene that plays on the TV. A man and a woman kissing in the rain. I started crying. 180 days, 10 hours, and 44 seconds, that's how long it has been since the end of our life.

"Are you sure you want to do this?" Ryan asked me. I smiled at him and kissed him on the cheek.

"Do you remember our vows?" He nodded. "Through thick and thin we will be with each other." We held hands and got on the bus together. We got to camp and went to our dormitories and rested because we both knew it would be a long day tomorrow.

"Training was an absolute hell," Ryan said. I nodded and put my head on his shoulder.

"But at least we survived," I said as he smiled at me. We hugged each other and went back to our rooms.

It was our first day in the trenches. All I remember is the smell of smoke and all the dead bodies. I was in the very back of the trench, popping up and down, shooting who I could. I got down again to reload, and I stayed there for a bit. One of the women got up ready to shoot, and all I heard was a big bang as she fell back with a giant hole in her head. I started crying. She was my bunkmate. I was stuck there for a week. When I got back, I went straight to the shower. After I got dressed, I snuck into his room and cuddled him.

"I don't know how much longer I can take this," I said to him. He looked at me and petted my hair.

"In a few months this will all be over." He lifted my chin. "We'll be fine."

We'll be fine.

That sentence still haunts me. I held the blanket tightly until my hands were white. I wasn't brave enough then, but I was now. I threw the blanket on the floor and went to the basement. I sat on the floor and waited for something to happen. The door shut. I moved my head around the room to see if anyone was there. Nothing. But then I heard a record scratch. I got up and went over to the sound and found an old phonograph with a record starting to play. "Four men in uniform / To carry home my little soldier."

"What could he do? Should have been a rock star."

"But he didn't have the money for a guitar."

"What could he do? Should have been a politician."

"But he never had a proper education."

"What could he do? Should have been a father."

"But he never even made it to his twenties."

"What a waste, army dreamers."

I slowly backed away from it as it continued to play. I began shaking. What was doing this, I wondered. *"Who are you?"* I signed. I heard a creak in the walls. I walked over to it. There was then another creak that lasted a little longer. Then there was another solid creak. Then I sat on the ground and tapped on it, asking it to repeat the first part. Whatever it was, repeat it. I started crying. R-Y-A-N. I curled myself in a ball and continued to bawl.

I woke up in my bed and I turned around to my nightstand to find a vase full of daisies. My breathing started to get heavy. How did they get there? Was I going crazy? This had to be an episode, right? Right? I headed to my door to get to the kitchen, but the door wouldn't open. I twisted several times. I banged my body against the door, but it still wouldn't budge. *"Why are you doing this to me?"*

"Because you didn't save me." He reached for the—

My eyes shot open, and I fell out of bed. My breathing was heavy. I went back to the bed and hid under the covers. I didn't know what to do. I decided to text Clara.

"Hello," I said. "Hi."

"Is everything going okay?"

"What's the history of this house?"

"It used to be an Army hospital," she texted. "Why?"

"My episodes are getting worse."

"I'm coming over!"

"Can you come over later?"

"Ok."

I walked back to the door. It finally opened, and I walked back to the living room. I heard creaks on the wall, but I didn't pay attention to what he was saying. I started crying again. My whole back and face got cold. *"I love you,"* I signed. Then I paid attention to the creaks.

"I love you too," the code continued, "but you have to let me go."

"I can't." He didn't say anything. I heard a knock on the door. I answered it.

"I know you said later, but I needed to make sure you were okay." I hugged Clara right away and started crying. She hugged me back and rubbed my back. I felt this heavy weight start getting off my chest. After that I invited her in and explained everything.

"Wow, that's a lot to take in," Clara said. I looked at her ashamedly. I'm supposed to be stronger than this. Before I was able to spiral deeper, Clara touched my hand. "Stop, I know what you are doing." Clara sighed. "Overthinking this is going to make it worse." I nodded.

"*Am I crazy?*" I signed.

Clara looked at me with a surprised look on her face. "No, why would you even think that?" she said.

"*No normal person sees the ghost of their dead husband,*" I signed.

"A person who was not allowed to grieve for six months might."

I was speechless. Had it really been that long?

"Or there could be a ghost. I won't take anything off the table."

I smiled. It was a genuine one too. "*I'm going to tell you what happened to Ryan.*"

Clara looked at me with a concerned look. "Are you sure?" she said.

I nodded and began telling her.

"We'll be alright, Ryan," I said to him. He shook his head.

"How do you know that?" He looked straight into my eyes.

I kissed him. "Because we're together," I said, "and together we can do anything."

He smiled at me. "I should tell you something. I got us a house before we left."

I hugged him tightly. "Was this supposed to be the birthday surprise you were telling me about?"

"It's not my fault. I thought we were supposed to be off."

I laughed at him. "Well, I should probably get back to my post."

He grabbed my hand and spun me around, and he kissed me. "I'll see you tomorrow," he told me.

We were both out in the field avoiding getting shot. "Grenade me," I told him. He passed it to me. I took the pin out and threw the grenade as far as I could. It got many of the soldiers that were shooting at us. I started breathing heavily.

Ryan noticed and put his hands on my face. "It's okay. We got them."

I shook my head. "They had families!" I screamed at him. "None of this is okay!"

"Remember what they told us," he said. "They are the enemy."

"They're doing the same job as us," I said.

"We have to make it home, no matter what."

I looked at him. What has this job done to him? I thought. We got to a safer place and calmed down.

"Once this is all over, I'm going to give you the future you wanted for us."

I smiled knowing the image I told him on our fifth date. A two-story house with fruit trees and a garden and enough room for pets to play.

"Sounds perfect." I kiss him on the cheek. "Let's keep moving." We moved across the field. I saw little bumps in the ground, and I put my arm out and pointed them out.

He nodded.

"We just have to be really careful." I took his hand and squeezed it.

We began walking down a path. We were about halfway out when we heard a gun going off. We still stayed on the right part of the path. We looked at each other and we nodded. He went on the land mine path just out of reach of touching them. He waved his hands up. The sniper took a shot, and Ryan dived out of the way and took me down with him. My ears were ringing. "Ryan, are you okay?" I asked. I heard a few coughs.

"Yeah, just peachy," he said, and I slapped his shoulder. We continued walking again and men jumped us. I elbowed my guy, but he was so strong. He got a knife and just as he was starting to cut me, he was flung off me by Ryan. He started punching him. I slowly got up and got my gun out to shoot the attacker, but my trigger wasn't working. I went to reload, but then I heard a scream. I looked up and saw Ryan was stabbed. Tears started going down my face. Without wasting a second, I shot the attacker in the head. I ran over to Ryan and put pressure on the wound. He grabbed my hand and looked at me with tears in his eyes.

"I love you."

I shook my head. "We're going to make it," I said. His hands loosened and dropped to the ground. "No!"

"*It was my fault he died,*" I signed while I cried.

Clara grabbed my hand. "It wasn't your fault. You couldn't have possibly known that gun was unloaded."

"*I should have known,*" I signed. "We're always supposed to check."

"Do you think he would blame you?" she asked. I shook my head. "Then it's time to let you forgive yourself." I cried for what seemed like hours. When my tears finally dried up, I heard a creak and the front door was slightly open. I smiled at that.

"*Do you want to get out of the shoebox?*" I signed. Clara smiled at me.

Clara just moved in this week, and I couldn't be happier. Ryan, my love, I think he's moved on to a happier place. I still miss him a lot. I finally got to a doctor and got medication and a therapist. She's also an army vet and helps me out a lot. Could this all have been in my head? Maybe, but I like to think Ryan is out there helping others.

"Hey, there you are," Clara said. "Supper's done, when you're ready."

"Okay. I'll be in in a minute."

She nodded.

This is a fresh start, and I'm not going to waste it.

The Echoes of Annesley

AJ FASTNACHT

Just outside of a town named Annesley, there was a woman who lived alone. She was a mother to a man named Damian. The woman loved Damian and refused to let him leave the house when he wanted to move out. Damian did not want to spend another day in that house of hers. He often talked about how awful it was to have lived there for so long already. The lady would worship the devil all day and all night long. She would host satanic rituals in the basement of the house. She invited many demons and spirits into the house that traumatized Damian. He couldn't wait to move out of the house.

Not many other people in the town knew of what she did behind closed doors. Damian was not allowed to talk about that when he left the front door. They lived in a small, very run-down subdivision that is located next to an abandoned cemetery. The other people who lived in this subdivision were also devil worshipers. Once a month, everyone in this secluded subdivision got together at night in the cemetery and held satanic rituals. On these nights, Damian would stay home and lock himself in his room. He thought it would keep the spirits away, and he would be safe.

One day, Damian went to school like usual, but his teachers grew suspicious of him. They said that he was not acting like himself in the slightest. His teacher called the nurse and told her that Damian was headed down there. Once there she examined him and noticed something off. She got a chill down her spine and suddenly got extremely nauseous. She had never experienced this before and called the principal into the office. He had the same responses as the nurse. Growing suspicious of what was wrong with the boy and not knowing what else to do, they called a priest. The priest came to examine the boy and told the principal to dismiss school early. School got out right after lunch time, and all the teachers were ordered to rush the students out of the building. None of the parents knew what was happening and were told that they would be updated by sundown.

The priest had to perform an exorcism on Damian. He was possessed by an evil spirit. The purification of his soul took more than four hours. Because of the demon exorcism that had to happen, Damian was late coming home. His mother probed him as to why he was so late. He explained to her what happened, and she scolded him. He didn't understand why she was so upset. If he had kept the demon inside of him for too long, it would have killed him. She screamed and told him that he was a disgrace and, "you do not dishonor the devil like that." He stormed off to his room and cried all night. Later that night, a ghost came to comfort him. She was super nice and wasn't there to hurt him. She was there to help him. She kind of looked like his mother but softer. She told him that he had to get rid of his mother and the rest of this small cult. He listened to the ghost and devised a plan to get rid of the cult. First, he started with his mother. He grabbed a kitchen knife and slit her throat in her sleep and watched her bleed out. He felt a sense of satisfaction after doing so. He felt freedom for the first time in his life. He then went around house to house and did the same to the rest of the psychos around the neighborhood. After everyone was dead, he buried all the bodies in the cemetery.

Damian then lived on his own for a while, basking in his new-found freedom. He waited until school was almost out to make his next move. He would burn down the houses. Since it was spring and all the surrounding farmers were notorious for burning their fields, he started burning them down one by one. He started at dusk and let them burn all night long. By morning, all the smoke had cleared. The next night Damian would burn another one down, and so on and so on until they were all gone. He then fled town. Never returned to school and never saw his friends again.

A couple weeks later as the surrounding farmers started planting crops, they noticed the houses were gone and all turned to ash. They called the police and alerted them of the arson that was committed. They found nothing and ruled it a mystery. They never found the bodies of the residents that lived there.

A few years went by, and Damian returned to town to see an old friend from high school. He tried to return to where the houses were, but the road was closed off.

He turned off his car and got out to walk around the barricades. He couldn't see much, so he just left. Upon leaving, his car wouldn't start. The engine stalled for two more tries. It finally started on the third try. He just got a brand-new car, so he was puzzled as to why it was stalling already. Driving off he heard noises outside but thought nothing of it. He kept hearing them, so he pulled over and rolled down his windows. All he heard were faint screams. He left thinking about what he had done to his mother and the rest of the neighborhood.

That night he went home and sat in silence for hours, replaying what had happened years ago. He finally went to bed. Nightmares ensued and kept waking him up. He couldn't take it: the nightmares, the flashbacks, the regret. He woke up for the last time at 3 am. He decided to go out the same way he took out his mother. The knife dragged across his throat, and he felt the blood gushing out of him.

GRACE HARTMAN

Unknown Address

It was like a place stuck in time. Dour and conspicuous, and yet reserved into the shadows of the trees above. It could have been beautiful, if it were not so unnerving; if its very unblemished, antique perfection were not such a seeming anomaly. Because it stood, unmoving, while, like the breeze through the leaves, the world around it shifted little by little.

It was not difficult to name it the "haunted house"; it so perfectly fit the image of one. Sat quaintly at a corner, it was dark-colored and dreary if neatly built and trimmed. But its garden, large and fenced, was beautiful. That was one symptom of its strange stillness; that such a garden, blossoming and verdant, could stay maintained without the slightest trace of human touch. In the middle was a young, skinny tree, and in the spring, it would blossom pink, unlike any other tree around.

I knew it because I saw it each and every day. I saw it from my childhood school, from the swings and play-set, its back window and garden; from the journey to and from home, its profile and shadowy front porch. It was the old house, the ugly house, the dark house; the abandoned house. And that was the key: its abandonment, its lack of life and human activity, its stillness through time and change and season. But it *was not* abandoned, not in the way it ought to have been. There were no boarded windows and broken glass, no peeling paint and unhinged shutters, no weedy gardens and foreclosure signs. It did not sit at the end of a street, at a dead end, with only wild grass and trees beyond it and the cruelty of time defacing it. It sat in a neighborhood, at a corner, by a school full of growing children, by houses that changed every year.

Through those windows little could be seen: a lamp, a chair, a vase of poinsettias. The back window, overlooking the garden and the schoolyard beyond it, possessed three odd decorations. Three small statuettes of hands, beginning from the forearm, two colored obsidian and the other alabaster, sat on their stumps, reaching upwards.

I thought up a story about those hands, about that house. A way to, in my mind, solidify *why* that house should be a haunted house. Why it stood the way it did, creepy and unstirring, with no signs of life. Because there had to be something *inside of there;* that was the reason.

The story centered on a child, like me, watching a haunted house from their schoolyard, like me. They were bolder or stupider, or perhaps just prone to worse luck, than me, because unlike me, they managed to get inside the house. For them, however, that spelled out misfortune. The owner, so elusive it was questionable that they even existed, was a witch. And true to childhood fears, she was the kind that turned children into animals and made them into stew.

I can't quite remember the ending. My mind was fixed on those three statuettes, I know, and my story served to answer that question too.

I think another child had fallen victim to her too, and had been turned into a black cat, true to folk stories about familiars. And now this new victim would too.

But the statuettes—they were those hands, half transmogrified into the paws of a black cat. Those were the obsidian ones. And the alabaster one, in some play of cruelty, was the cut off vestige of the child's humanity.

Had it been two black hands, one white? Or was it the other way around? I can't remember. I can't remember because I can't see it anymore. Because time did march on, in a way, finally. But not in a way that was satisfying.

My childhood school was no longer a school. Something I wanted to keep the same changed. Time moved on without me, without it.

And time took the house—a little. To a point that would have been jarring at one time, but now, having creeped up, was barely noticed. The lack of human touch and care finally showed its mark. Plants overgrown, paint peeling. Just barely. Just slightly.

In a decade and more in which lives changed, children grew, and schools closed their doors, it had moved an inch, and did not show its hand while doing so. Of course, even its slight abandonment could show no signs of human life.

It made me mad. It vexed me, how something could stay in one's eyeline, stay in one's periphery, and not blink once. And if I blinked, I had no answers for how things became the way they did.

The tall grass lining the sidewalks was mocking. The peeling taupe stucco high up on the second story was mocking. The bushes, wild like kudzu, crawling up the walls, blocking the windows, were mocking. The pink-blossoming tree, wrapped in vines that choked it into leaflessness, was mocking. It let time pass at the expense of blocking all inquiries inside. It revealed a trick and then guarded itself. It let me blink to forget what I should be watching for, and then barred me seeing what had changed.

It could not let itself be exempt from time. It could not keep watching things wither and change and mysteriously, inexplicably, not. It was so smug as to exist in a way that seemed implausible and still to deny answers.

I could not take it. I could not look at still swing sets and dead saplings and be denied looking through windows I'd watched for ten years.

The anger took me. It took me up the sidewalk path, split at the corner curb and leading up like an arrow. It took me to the dark wooden porch, and the dark front door, and to the dark, black doorknob. My hand took it, and it turned. It pushed and slid open easily, like it was somehow in regular use.

The house was not lit. Why would it be? Light from outside, that which could break through the leaves crowding the windows, was the only source. Dust motes floated through the faint beams. Flickers of dust particles, the shifting of leaves, but beyond that, stillness.

Each step made something creak. At each movement, dust swirled in the air. The air was thick with it. It was thick and stuffy, the opening of the door like the opening of a crypt. That airflow was all that made it possible to scarcely breathe in there. The summer heat made it worse still. Even with a shallowness of breath, I moved further in.

It took me to the window, to the chair I had seen years ago. Like my memory, it was old, an antique, something that ought to have belonged to a house such as this. When I touched it, it felt so firm as to have never been used before. The vase of poinsettias accompanied it. Artificial, of course; never blooming nor wilting like everything else in the house. Its faux petals had turned from blood to rust in the layers of dust.

I took to the stairs, each step a warning to whatever might be in there to come out, come clean. But nothing was there.

The lamp I saw on dark winter mornings in the upstairs window was on. I marveled at it. The one sign of life, it always felt automated. It was on a timer, I had surmised. But I never knew why. For what appearances?

But for every light switch in the house I had come upon and flicked, nothing had happened. I looked for this light's, too, and found it, but the result was much the same. It stayed on. I touched the bulb, and it was cold.

The place I wanted to see the most was the back window. I wanted to remember what the statuettes were like. I wanted to see the disarray of the garden up close. I found it, beyond a door, like all kitchens used to be. Everything divided, able to be kept shut by a door or wall. But I found the window, because I could see the light spilling in from outside. I could see the statuettes, two coupled together, one an outlier, but I was distracted by what I saw beyond them.

There were no leaves obscuring the window now. I could see freely, fully. I saw the schoolyard full of children. I could feel the slick material of old jackets and the fabric knots on pairless gloves. I knew it was not now. I knew exactly when it was.

The now overgrown and dead garden was blooming and lush again, and in the middle, the skinny young tree blossomed pink.

Listen to the Ghost

ELIANA HOGAN

Opening the car door, Elodie stepped into the parking garage with one of her suitcases in tow. She had finally gotten an apartment so that she could begin living on her own. After checking in with the owner of the complex, she got her garage opener and the key to her apartment. Before she walked into the building, she also grabbed a second suitcase so that all her clothing would at least be in the building at the same time.

Walking into the building, she got to the elevator and realized it was out of order. Not the biggest inconvenience, but it was not going to be fun walking up the stairs to the third floor several times throughout the day just to get stuff to her apartment. She started her trek up the stairs with the first of many things, when a man came walking down the stairs. "Do you want some help, ma'am?" he offered as soon as he saw Elodie struggling to get both suitcases up the stairs.

"Yes, please, if you don't mind."

In response, he grabbed both the suitcases and allowed Elodie to lead the way up the stairs.

"I'm Job by the way. I live on the fifth floor." That was his way of breaking the awkward silence that occurred when Elodie was getting the key to open her door.

"I'm Elodie. I live ..." The sentence petered out because she realized how silly it was of her to tell him that she lived on the third floor.

"I'm assuming you have a lot more to bring up? I can help you if you need it."

That was music to her ears, but she felt like she had to decline because she didn't want to burden the man.

"Trust me, Ms. Elodie, I want to help you," was his response.

Throughout the rest of the morning, Elodie and Job made the trip up and down the stairs a total of 10 more times. After they got all of her possessions into her apartment, they both took a much deserved breather. "Let me get you some lunch, Job. It's the least I can do for all your help." Elodie offered lunch to people a lot.

She liked to make sure that the people around her had eaten, since she knew what it was like when you don't eat.

"I would appreciate that, although, can we order it in? I don't know if I want to walk down those stairs again." The two people shared a laugh, and then decided what they would have delivered.

Job ended up staying in Elodie's apartment a lot longer than he had intended. Elodie realized he had been in there for at least four hours, even after they finished eating their food. Eventually, he did have to take his leave because now he did have something he needed to do. What that was, he never told Elodie, but that was alright with her because they were still relative strangers.

Elodie had moved around a lot as a kid, and the one thing she picked up from those experiences was that the second day in a new place was for unpacking everything. So that is what she did. She had just started when there was a knock at her door. Walking towards the door with some trepidation, she looked through the peephole and realized it was Job. "Oh, hi, Job. What are you doing here?" She was curious as to why the man would come back a second time as that was another thing she had little to no experience with.

"Well, I figured you would be unpacking, so I thought I would come help you." He held out his hands, and in them were two bottles of sparkling grape juice. She had told Job the night before that she didn't like to drink alcohol, and that her favorite alternative was sparkling grape juice.

"Well, thank you! I'm never going to turn down help." That whole day was spent unpacking and drinking sparkling grape juice from wine glasses so as to appear "more adultish." They again ordered food and spent the rest of the night talking.

Elodie was beginning to feel some kind of romantic feeling toward Job. She knew that was ridiculous because they had known each other for only two days. *This man has helped me the last two days, though. Not many men would do that nowadays, would they?* Her thoughts had been consumed by Job in the hours that she didn't spend with him, and now that they were eating another meal together, she thought she may be reading too much into what she was seeing. At around 8 pm, Job left again, saying that he had something that he needed to do. As he was standing in the door, he said to Elodie, "We should have dinner at my place tomorrow. I am a good cook. 6:45 if that works for you." Elodie agreed to the dinner, saying that she would bring up a small dish just so that it felt like she made a contribution to the dinner.

Job did not visit her in the morning. They had exchanged numbers the day they met, and he told her that he was going to spend the entire day preparing the dinner. So Elodie started to think about what she wanted to make for dinner. Eventually she decided that she wanted to make cinnamon rolls. She had some frozen premade rolls in her freezer, so she got them out around 10 am so they could thaw before going in the oven. While they were doing this, Elodie decided to sit at the breakfast bar that separates her living room and kitchen and do some reading. This was a book she easily got lost in, so she had to set a timer to check on the thawing cinnamon rolls. Once they were sufficiently thawed, she put them in the oven around 2 pm and had them bake slowly so that by the time she was ready to go to supper with Job, they would be warm. She sat down with her book at the breakfast bar and got lost in her reading.

All at once, something came to her. She couldn't remember how or why it started, but suddenly she was not in her apartment anymore. She was standing in what seemed to be an empty room, save for another woman standing at the opposite end and a grandfather clock that read 3 pm. The woman was dressed in what appeared to be rags, but upon further inspection, Elodie saw they were funeral clothes. Burial clothing at that. Elodie began to tremble, for she knew nothing about what was happening to her.

As her trembling reached a high, she suddenly heard a sound. She assumed it was a voice, but anytime it tried to speak, it came out garbled. Elodie tried to approach the woman at the other end of the room to see if she was the one making the noise. At every step she took towards the woman, though, the room appeared to elongate, as if telling her that she shouldn't move forward. Out of nowhere, the room shrank, and she was suddenly face to face with the woman. And as she looked in this woman's eyes, she realized the worst. This woman was dead, and she wasn't just pretending.

"Who are you?" Elodie whispered. She could not yell, as there was some supernatural force pressing upon her, preventing her from doing anything of the sort. There was no response, so she studied the ghost's face. Her pupils were dilated, her lips were blue, and she had something on the corner of her mouth that resembled dry vomit. Elodie asked her question again: "Who are you?" There wasn't much of a response, but this time she did respond with one word … "Run."

As Elodie began to consider what she was told, the room became normal again, and she was standing in her kitchen. *What the hell was that?* she thought. Nothing like that had ever happened to her before, at least not at the house she lived in with her parents. She decided to brush it off. She was just stressed from the move. She had never lived on her own before, so that had to be it. Stress. The answer to everything for her was just stress. Then she realized that she had food in the oven and scrambled to make sure it wasn't burned. Visions like this persisted throughout the entire day, and when she was almost late to dinner with Job, she decided she was going to ask someone about it later. She always had later.

She took her cinnamon rolls out of the oven so that they had a little bit of time to cool, and so that she could put the frosting on them. As she was doing this, she heard the voice again. It wasn't a full vision, but she heard the voice. "Don't go. Run," was all it said. Elodie was starting to get extremely annoyed. There was no context behind what the voice was telling her. Why would it be telling her to run? Run from whom or what? These visions were annoying at best. Putting the warning into the back of her head, she left her apartment and started the trek up the stairs towards Job's apartment.

She knocked only once before Job opened the door. His apartment smelled of pork, potatoes, and homemade bread. As he led her into his apartment, she began to see the whole dinner spread that he had made. There were four pork chops laid out in the center of the table ready to be divvied out, a large bowl of mashed potatoes with chives sitting next to the pork chops, and some fresh dinner rolls sitting on top of the stove. "This is a lot of food for two people," Elodie remarked.

"I've been told that I am a good cook, so I figured I would make extra in case you wanted to take some with you back to your apartment after we are done here." Job was trying to woo Elodie with this statement.

"Well, it smells amazing, Job. I'm sure whoever told you that wasn't lying."

As Elodie sat down, Job began fixing drinks in the kitchen. From where she was sitting, she couldn't see what he was doing, but that didn't really bother her. What did bother her was the fact that she kept on hearing that same voice in the back of her head screaming "RUN. IT'S NOT TOO LATE." She kept pushing this voice to the back of her head, as if trying to lock it in a soundproof box so that she could no longer hear it. The voice finally quieted down when Job turned the corner with two glasses of wine in his hands. He handed the one in his right hand to Elodie and took the one in his left for himself.

The dinner went off without a hitch. The wine was delicious, and so was the food. The night was winding down, so Elodie excused herself to go back to her apartment. That would be the last time she ever walked anywhere.

She began to feel slightly tired, so she went to lie down in her bed. As she tried to sleep, she began to feel nauseated. This turned into her throwing up a lot of what she had eaten just a few hours before. When she thought she was done, she went to lie back in her bed. This was her final mistake. She had one final bout of vomiting, but because it snuck up on her, she had no time to even sit up. She realized as she was lying in bed that she couldn't even move without feeling like she was hit by a bus. She was choking on her own puke, and because she couldn't try to sit herself up, she continued to choke until she could no longer breathe. Elodie took her final breath in agonizing pain, dying in her own bed.

When she opened her eyes again, she was in the same room where she had been having those visions. This time, though, the woman in the corner was a lot clearer, and she could see that what she was wearing wasn't old, ragged funeral clothes, but torn up clothing. "I told you that you needed to run, yet you didn't listen to me. Now you are like me, and together hopefully we can stop the next victim." The woman's voice was so much clearer now.

"Next victim? What do you mean?" Elodie was confused.

"You and I both died at the hands of that man. Job is a terrible man. Did you wonder why it took so long for him to come out with the drinks? He was putting eyedrops in your wine."

It all made sense now. She had heard of stories about this happening to other people. "How do you know that is what happened to you?" Elodie was confused. If this ghost that she was talking to was telling the truth, how did she know that that is how she died?

"I'm not the first person this has happened to. Every single person that has moved into your apartment has been killed by Job. You are the fifth."

All this information weighed heavily on Elodie. Now she realized that she has the same mission as the ghost sitting in front of her. A few months later, another young woman was moving into the building, and the cycle started again. Elodie and the ghost were hoping this woman would listen to them, but it didn't seem like that was going to happen.

Alone at the Cabin

BREADEN HUFFORD

It was a nice fall evening and there were two boys playing catch in the backyard of a little home up in the mountains. The family rented a cabin because one of the boys had a camp they were going to. The older boy named Brenner loved baseball. It was his passion in life. The younger brother named Brighton loved wrestling. It was his passion in life. It was Brenner's senior year of high school, so he was getting ready for his final year of high school baseball.

Brenner was getting scouted and recruited throughout his career, so he was determined to play college ball. His brother wanted to pursue wrestling in college, so he was going to camps and a bunch of school visits everywhere. Brighton had a wrestling camp the next day, and the whole family was going to go visit the college with him. However, Brenner decided to stay back because he had a baseball tournament that weekend, and he wanted to train and be ready for it. It was getting late, so the boys decided to head inside and get ready for bed, because they had a big day ahead of them.

The next day came, and Brighton and the rest of the family were headed off to the wrestling camp. Brighton was ecstatic and pumped. He felt this coach would really like him. They got in the car and started their journey. Brenner then got to work. He got in the cage and began training to be the best he could be. He spent the whole day working out and practicing his craft.

The fall night soon came, and the dark came quickly. Since they were up in the mountains, the night got kind of foggy. Brenner decided to clean up and get ready for bed. He hopped in the shower, and the hot water made the room steam up. As he got out of the shower, he went to wipe the mirror to see himself. He was combing his hair, and he accidentally knocked one of the shampoo bottles off the sink. He bent down to pick it up but as soon as he stood up he saw something move in the mirror and it startled him. Brenner had no idea what it was, but he thought he was just seeing things. It was Brenner's first night home alone. He looked at the clock and it said

11 pm. Brenner had a long day, so he was exhausted. As soon as his head hit that pillow he was out.

An hour went by, and Brenner was awoken by the sound of the shower in the bathroom. He was a little freaked out, but he was super tired and just thought that he was dreaming so he went back to sleep. After about 5 minutes the shower turned off, and the house was dead silent. Brenner was sound asleep but then the shower turned back on again, so he decided to go investigate.

Brenner was thinking it could be an intruder or it was just a malfunction with the water pipes that made the shower turn on; he had no idea, and he wasn't going to take any chances. Brenner grabbed his baseball bat in his room and turned on every single light in sight. As he slowly walked towards the bathroom his heart-beat started to grow faster and faster. Step by step the wood floors in the cabin would creak and as Brenner approached the bathroom the shower shut off.

After the day Brenner had, he was trying really hard to stay awake during this. Since the shower turned off, he decided to go back to his room and go to bed. As soon as Brenner turned his body, he felt a gust of wind brush against his shoulder, and he got chills that ran down the back of his spine. This really woke him up, and he was terrified at this point. This made him remember what he saw in the mirror after his shower. Brenner put the pieces together and he knew that there was something in the cabin with him. He tried to keep his composure and stay calm, but he had no idea what to do. He wasn't going to fight this thing because he didn't know what it was. Brenner made the choice to go back to bed in hopes that he would wake up the next morning. His eyes were bloodshot, and he was still very tired from the day he had. He went to bed with his baseball bat to defend himself in the event that he was attacked.

The sun came up the next morning, and Brenner woke up and got out of bed totally fine, like nothing had happened. His family came back from the wrestling camp, and he greeted them outside. Brighton told Brenner all about the camp and that the coach loved him and offered him a scholarship. So after all the ruckus through the dark night everything seemed to work out just fine and Brenner decided to keep what happened to him to himself.

The Haunted Trip to Turks and Caicos

ABBY KLATT

It was the summer of 2021. Abby and her family were going on a vacation to Turks and Caicos. They thought it was going to be a fun and thrilling trip, but it wasn't all that it seemed to be. They didn't know what lay ahead of them. They didn't think they were going to make it out of that trip alive.

School had just gotten out for summer vacation. During the middle of June, the family usually went on vacation somewhere. This year a vacation was much needed by the family, especially Abby. The COVID-19 pandemic was still going on, and she was adjusting to changes at her new school. Her grandmother, who always wore bright red lipstick, had also died during this time, after a long illness. Abby's family was made up of four people: her older sister Emily, her mother Melanie, and her father James. The family decided a resort on the island of Turks and Caicos would be a great vacation.

The flight to the island was leaving at four in the morning, so the family decided it would be best to stay in a hotel in Omaha the night before.

The family drove to Omaha and planned on staying in the Country Inn and Suites. They hadn't heard any bad reviews about Country Inn and Suites, so they thought it would be a nice and comfy stay. Turns out they were wrong. They didn't know what terrifying thing was coming their way.

When they arrived at their room, they found a drawer left open. They didn't suspect anything at the time, so they just closed the drawer and went on with their normal activities. Everything was going as planned: they went out for supper and then came back to swim in the hotel's pool. When they came back from the pool, they noticed the drawer popped open again. They thought it was just a faulty drawer, so they shut it again.

Everyone went to bed since it would be a very early morning. They were all peacefully sleeping, when all of a sudden the alarm started blaring in their ears. That meant it was time to get the show on the road. They all

did their morning routines and grabbed their luggage
and were out the door. They went downstairs to meet
up with the shuttle driver who would take them to the
airport.

Abby was awfully tired. She had gotten only a few
hours of sleep. Abby, being last to board the shuttle, saw
a shadow by the passenger door. The shadow looked like
an older woman wearing stiletto high heels and bright
red lipstick, and she had a veil covering her face. Abby
thought she was hallucinating that shadow because of
her lack of sleep. She tried to forget what she saw and
got into the shuttle. The family was off to the airport.

All the required paperwork and procedures were
done, and they were off to Turks and Caicos. The plane
ride was going to take five hours, so the whole family
tried to get some rest. When the family woke up, they
realized they were just a few minutes away from their
destination. When the plane finally landed. Abby and
her family made it to their summer vacation spot to get
some rest and relaxation.

When they got off the plane, they felt the change in
weather right away. It was really humid and warm. It was

way different than Nebraska weather. After they grabbed their luggage, they rode to the resort on a shuttle. The resort had great reviews by past visitors, and it was right by the ocean. Every person in the family loved to go to the beach, so this was a great pick for the vacation.

When they arrived at the resort, they were greeted by the Islanders that worked there. Turks and Caicos is located near Cuba and considered part of the Caribbean region. Most of the people who work at the resort are of African descent. Their culture is displayed through colorful clothing and their accents, and most of them have cornrow braids in their hair. Staff members were very friendly and welcoming to the family.

Abby and her family looked around the resort before heading up to their room. Their first stop was the beach. The beach had white sand that was as soft as silk and crystal-clear blue water. After they went to the beach, they walked around the resort. The resort had many palm trees and flowers. The palm trees and flowers are alive during the whole year, since it is always warm there. After they looked around the resort, they thought it was a good idea to go to their room.

They were on the fifth floor, which was the top floor of the resort. The resort had no elevators, so they climbed all of those flights of stairs. When they opened the door to their room, they noticed something they had noticed at Country Inn and Suites in Omaha: a drawer was open. Not only was a drawer open, but it was open in the exact same spot as the drawer in Omaha. Abby's parents thought it was just a coincidence, but Abby had become suspicious of the whole situation. Her parents told her that she shouldn't suspect anything about that drawer being open and that she should just enjoy the vacation. Abby thought her parents were right, but she still kept her guard up. They shut the drawer and went on with their day.

Abby and her family went downstairs to get some supper. There were many restaurants at this resort, so it was hard for them to pick which restaurant they wanted to go to. They decided to go to a delicious Italian restaurant. After they finished eating, they headed upstairs to their room. It took them a while to get to their room because they were all stuffed from that gigantic meal.

When they opened the room door, Abby noticed that the drawer had popped open again and inside was a tube of bright red lipstick. She knew something wasn't right. Abby shut the door before her family could get in. Her heart was beating so fast that it felt like it was going to explode out of her chest. Abby's mother asked her what was wrong. Abby told her family that she thought their room was haunted. Her father said to her that ghosts aren't real, so the room surely wasn't haunted. Her father then opened the door again to see what Abby was talking about. He saw that the drawer was open again, but told Abby that it wasn't ghosts that have been opening the drawer. It was the faulty construction of the dresser.

As the family started getting ready for bed, Abby's heart was beating a million miles an hour. She asked her mother if they could move rooms. Her mom told her that would be crazy and that all the other rooms were full. Her mother told her to let go of the whole ghost nonsense and enjoy the vacation. Abby tried to let go of the whole ghost nonsense, but she just couldn't. She knew that the drawer popping open that many times wasn't just a coincidence. She knew some ghostly figure opened it. She was going to get to the bottom of it if it was the last thing she did.

There were only two beds, so Abby had to sleep with her sister. She knew that sleeping with her sister was already going to be a challenge, but now she had that worry in her stomach about a ghost coming during the middle of the night to possess her or even worse. She stayed up for a while, until her body finally told her that it was time for bed. She fell into a deep slumber.

Abby was sleeping well, until she wasn't. She woke up with a strange feeling in the pit of her stomach. When she fully opened her eyes, she saw that the drawer was open again. Her heart started to race. She pushed off the covers and got out of bed. After shutting the drawer, she started to pace back and forth to try to make sense of this situation. She kept thinking of what her father said about ghosts not being real and that maybe the dresser was poorly constructed. Her heart rate started to slow down a little. She started heading back for the bed, when all of a sudden she saw a shadowy figure on the balcony. It was the same shadowy figure she saw by the shuttle in Omaha. She ran to the balcony to see who it was. When she got onto the balcony, the shadowy figure was gone. She tried to make sense of all of this. She tried to trick herself into thinking that she was hallucinating from lack of sleep. She finally convinced herself that it was from lack of sleep and headed back to bed.

At 4:30 in the morning, everyone was sleeping again except for Emily, Abby's older sister. She got up from bed to use the restroom. When she came back, she looked at her phone for a while to help her fall back to sleep. When she put her phone down and lay down again, she heard Abby make weird sounds. Emily thought Abby was just having a nightmare, so she didn't do anything and tried to go back to sleep. The sounds started to get louder and louder. Emily knew that something wasn't right, so she woke up their parents. They all came and surrounded Abby. All of a sudden, Abby started to shake. Her mother tried to wake her up, but it was no use. She was in a deep sleep.

Emily then noticed a discoloration in Abby's skin tone. It started to turn pale, except for her lips. They were bright red. Their parents started to notice the discoloring too. They were all freaking out, when all of a sudden Abby sat up. Her eyes were bulging out of her head and her body was rocking. Emily asked Abby if she was awake. Abby didn't answer. Abby then started to scream in a trance that she wanted to go back. None of her family knew what she meant by that. After the trance ended, Abby lay back down and went back to sleep. When Abby laid her head on the pillow, the family saw a ghostly figure leave Abby's body. It was a lady-like figure who looked like she was at a loss in the world. After the ghost disappeared, they put their eyes back on Abby. Her mother tried to wake her up again. This time, she woke up.

Abby asked her family why they were all surrounding her. They were confused by that question because they thought she knew what just happened to her. Emily asked her if she knew what just occurred. Abby said that she didn't remember anything. The parents and Emily didn't want to freak her out, so they came up with an excuse for surrounding her. They told her that she was doing math in her sleep and that it was fascinating how many questions she was getting correct. She believed them, and they all went back to sleep.

In the morning, Abby and her family headed down to the breakfast buffet. No one mentioned anything about the strange events of the previous night while Abby was present. When she got up from the table for a second serving, her father turned to her mother and brought up the situation from last night. They knew it was not just a coincidence. They knew there was only one reason for such a situation: Abby was possessed last night by a ghost. They now believed that ghosts were real. When Abby came back to the table, her parents had come to a complete silence. They didn't want to tell Abby that she was right about ghosts being real, so they did not tell her about that night.

As the trip was coming to an end and the family started to pack their bags, Abby turned to her mother and father and told them they were right. She told them that it was silly to think ghosts were real. They could have told her that she was actually right about ghosts being real, but they didn't. They knew that if they told her, she would be angry with them. They just went along with what she said and said that they are happy that she let go of that ghost nonsense and had fun on the vacation.

During the shuttle ride to the airport, Abby noticed her parents' faces were unsettled. She asked them what was wrong. They had another chance to tell her about the possession, but they didn't. They just told her that they were sad the vacation was coming to an end. Abby believed them and told them she was sad it was coming to an end too.

The flight back to the great state of Nebraska was five hours long. Abby, Emily, and her father took a nap on the plane, while her mother read a book. When they landed at the Omaha airport, a shuttle took the family back to their car at the Country Inn and Suites and they headed home. As they all entered the house, Abby told her family they should go to Turks and Caicos again. The parents had one last chance to tell Abby about the possession, but they didn't. To this day, they have never mentioned it.

A Soldier's Ghost Story

PAIGE KUHN

I've never believed in the paranormal. In fact, I've never really believed in anything that I haven't experienced firsthand or that everyone knows for a fact to be true. But it's not for lack of trying. I wish more than anything that I could wholeheartedly believe in something, a greater being that watches over me, guiding me. However, it is, for lack of a better word, unfortunate that most of my experiences in life have been far from pleasant, causing me to doubt if there really is a greater being who's supposed to be watching over me. One event, years ago, challenged this doubt, though. I was stationed in the middle of a war zone in a foreign country with nothing to hold onto but my fear. My experiences in the war dimmed even that to a dull feeling in the back of my mind, however. It was on one of the more melancholy of my days spent overseas that I encountered something that even to this day I have no explanation for.

The week prior to this encounter my squad members had one of the worst days of our lives. We had just gotten back from a previous mission, out in the deserts of Iraq. It was a mission that ended in the misfortune of one of our brothers being lost to us forever, but we had no time to grieve because we had already been assigned another mission. Alas, that's how it always worked. They kept us busy, unable to have a moment to think, to breathe, to mourn. We were tin soldiers, with our only purpose to fight, sent out on mission after damn mission. In some ways I was grateful for that, for the distraction, but the stress and exhaustion could make even the toughest of soldiers go mad, make you see things, people, that weren't there.

This time our mission was to mortar an enemy house. It was nothing special. I've done tons of these types of missions before. However, this time when we rode up to the old, haunted-looking warehouse under the pale glow of the moon, there was an eerie bite to the air. I was hesitant this time. I had gotten so used to being a robot carrying out the missions without a second thought, but something was making me pause, like a rope tugging me in the opposite direction, urging me to turn my boots and run far away. I was startled out of my inner conflict—"Alright, boys, let's not drag this out. We all wanna get home at a decent hour," the commander overseeing all our missions said. If we soldiers were like brothers, then our commander was our father, overseeing and protecting us. His words spurred us into action, and we all took our posts. Mine was in the hutch above the truck where the mortar launched. I sat waiting to cause pain and loss. Under the dark night sky you could see shadows passing through the illuminated windows in the warehouse. The enemy was so close. All I could picture was the lives of the brothers lost to us at the hands of these evil men. A red hot rage consumed me at the thought of everyone I had lost here. On the commander's word we aimed and fired all our mortars mercilessly at the enemy warehouse.

It felt like hours had passed, but in reality it couldn't have been more than 20 minutes. My ears were still ringing, and smoke was still curling up from the rubble of the warehouse, filling the air and burning my lungs. I welcomed the burn while the rubble crunched under my combat boots. We were doing recon, making sure there were no survivors. I walked in a daze until my heavy boot thunked underneath me. My heart sank with the sound, and I saw a trap door peeking out from underneath the rubble. I kneeled, brushing away the remaining debris, and opened the door. With my gloved hand, I wafted away the smoke that filled my eyes and nose. When the smoke dispersed and I realized what was hidden under the trap door, it felt like my soul had left my body. There was a child, a little boy, under that door.

I couldn't breathe, couldn't hear, couldn't think. My body moved by itself, my arms reaching out to pick up the child and lay his small body on my lap. He was covered in dirt and soot, and something else—a sticky substance that ran all down one side of his body from his head. I had been in enough battles and seen enough death to know what blood looked like, even in the dark. The boy was weeping silently. Or was that me? I couldn't tell. He was cradling one side of his face, the side covered in blood, with his hands. I reached up to hold his hands in my own, hoping to stop his shivering, but when his hands fell away, part of his brain fell out with them. Half of his skull was gone, nothing but a dark bloody hole now. I tried to cry out, but my throat was clogged. The little boy stopped shivering, and I knew he had passed.

I'm not sure how long I stayed there like that, just holding his small frame, my tears dripping onto his blood-stained chest. Eventually I felt an arm on my shoulder pulling me from my grief. "There's nothing you can do now, son," the commander said, his voice full of dread. I nodded my head and shrugged off his hand, sniffling. I got up, still holding the boy close to my chest. I walked us to the end of the rubble and gently set his body to the side while I used a piece of metal lying on the ground to turn up the soil, making a makeshift grave. Tears still leaked from my eyes, leaving tracks in the dirt on my cheeks. Trying not to move his body too much, in fear of causing him more pain, as if he could still feel anything, I gently set the little boy in the grave and covered his body, laying him to rest. I laid a make-shift cross across his grave, in hopes that if there was a higher up being, they would guide his soul to peace.

A week passed, and not one day went by where I didn't think of the little boy who died in my arms. I was distraught, I couldn't focus on anything, and every time I closed my eyes I saw his face. He was haunting my dreams even when I was awake. However, I needed to move on and stay focused. We were assigned another mission: recon on a new enemy base. We were gearing up, getting four different trucks ready to take out for the mission, when the commander approached me. "You sure you're good to be going out there right now, son?" he asked.

I took a long breath, steadying my nerves while he eyed me. "Yes, sir. I'm fine."

I must've not been convincing enough because he responded, "Look, boy, I know you're still rattled about … what happened. You say the word and I'll sit you out this round."

I appreciated his concern of course, but I needed the distraction. Sitting out wouldn't do me any good. "Thank you, sir," I said, "but I need to go tonight." The commander sighed but nodded firmly and walked away to finish preparing for the mission.

The gravel road we were driving on was rough and jostled our trucks aggressively. I was in the second truck, sitting in the passenger seat and keeping a look out for any suspicious activity. The explosion happened before any of us could register what was happening. The lead truck blasted at least 10 feet into the air, landing on its side and immediately burning up in flames. Another explosion went off, closer this time, hitting my truck. My vision blurred. My ears were ringing loudly yet I could still vaguely make out the screams of my brothers around me. As my vision went in and out of focus, I saw one of my brothers, the one who was driving the truck, slouched in his seat with a giant piece of shrapnel sticking out of his chest.

Panic set in, and I fumbled furiously to get out of the burning truck. Finally stumbling out, I looked back at the chaos, and through the fire and smoke a figure emerged. A small, familiar figure. The little boy that had passed in my arms was walking towards me, reaching for me. He looked like a normal boy this time. It was hard to make out specific features of him, like I was looking at him through a filter. But as he walked closer, I felt a sense of calm wash over me. He walked until he stood a breath away from me, then he reached out grasping my face between both of his hands and leaned down softly touching his forehead against mine. His touch was feather-light, almost nonexistent, but brought me the most comfort I had ever felt. I closed my eyes, accepting his comforting embrace. When I opened my eyes again the little boy was gone. And I was left wondering if I had truly gone mad or just experienced a taste of the paranormal I had fought so hard against.

The Bells

JAKE LAMBERT

Chapter 1

The sun was starting to set after the hot summer day. Laughing children could be heard from the woods. Marie was looking for a place to lay her head down in the garden. The sweet smell of dirt and earth filled her nose as she set down her clippers. She entered the garden every Saturday evening to count her plants and make sure they were all accounted for. Marie was thinking about looking at her new plants and taking them to the kitchen to be cooked later that night for supper. She had just gotten a new recipe for the lamb she planned on eating later.

Bryce had just gotten back from the general store in town and said, "How was your day, dear?"

He was kind to Marie, never angry and always happy to be with his kids. Marie had always liked him since she was introduced by her father. They were arranged to be married after Bryce graduated from college. He was very headstrong and made most of his money down at the pier.

"Just getting the last of the veggies for dinner tonight," she responded. Marie cooked almost every night.

She had no other options on what to do with her days. She stayed with her two young children, Lane and Poppy. Lane took after his father. He was the oldest and took care of his younger sister. He could have taken over the family job as soon as he was 3. It was like he had all the experience needed for life at a young age. Poppy was the spitting image of her mother, long dark blonde hair that curled right at the ends, her eyes were red with passion. She needed no one to take care of her.

Bryce looked towards the sound of laughing children. "Where are my little bees?" he shouted towards the woods.

The laughter stopped and the sound of buzzing started taking over the atmosphere. "Buzzzzzzz."

Lane was the first back and ran straight for his dad. "Next time take me with you," he said as he grabbed his father and took him in an embrace. Marie looked towards the woods. The sun was setting right in front of her eyes.

"Where's your sister?" Marie asked, looking around again.

"She was right behind me as we left," Lane said, turning around to face his mother.

Marie and her son were both very loving, and they loved each other, but Lane was scared of what she could do. When he was younger there was a time when he had gotten very sick. Nobody knew what to do and he was going to die. Later that week Lane got better and made a full recovery, but during this time his mother had almost killed him after drawing a bath and then drowning him while he was too weak to fight. She insisted she was not there and didn't remember the situation, but it had put this feeling of pain and betrayal in his heart. He couldn't help but smile in terror.

"Poppy!!" Marie called out.

No response. All of them together shouted, "Poppy!!" Still nothing.

There were a few cracks of branches, and leaves started rustling. Poppy emerged from the tree line shining from liquid covering her body. It was red, and Poppy was staring directly at Marie. She spoke but had two voices, her own and a voice not like the little girl's but like an older man. She said, "I'm still alive."

The voice seemed familiar to Marie. Then she heard bells.

Chapter 2

Marie's childhood was thrilling. When she was 4, she could see people no one else could. She first brought it up with her father. Someone was standing in the corner of the room when she told him. Her dad's face had a look of confusion and doubt as he turned to the same corner she was looking at. "I don't see anyone there, Marie. It's all in your head," he said with sincerity, trying to calm his daughter down. Marie could not look away from the tall slender figure standing in the corner. It was a man of some sort, but it had no face and no hair. Marie's encounters only grew from then on, more frequent and more intense.

One day, on a Sunday when Marie was much older, she decided to take a shortcut back through the woods when she was coming home from church. She lived about a 30-minute walk from the church. Her father had no horse or carriage so they would walk together. This Sunday her father had to stay late with the church to plan the big Easter event happening the next week. He sent Marie home and told her to be safe. Marie was just starting to experience being a woman and was told about her soon-to-be husband and how they would meet within the next year. Marie was walking through the woods when she came upon a huge grassy field. She knew she was close to home now, about 5 minutes away, and was ready to sit in the yard and read her new book. She was almost across the field when she heard something. *Dingaling adingaling.* She froze, unable to move.

Dingaling adingaling. Dingaling. There it was again. She snapped her neck. Turning around and looking through the open field, she saw no one around. She heard the sound again and again. Curiosity got the better of her and she started walking back into the middle of the field. She followed the bells, making her way closer as it got louder and louder. Eventually she was dead in the middle of the opening. The ringing stopped, and she looked around the tree line surrounding her. Not a bug could be heard making a chirp, the wind stopped blowing, and everything was still.

Three feet to her left was a stone, covered and surrounded by tall grass. It wasn't just a rock, though. It was a gravestone. She could see it was carved, and there was writing along the face of the stone. It read,

1848–1891

Here lies John Pierce,

died in peace sleeping.

Marie knew her dad got the house from the Pierce family. *John Pierce must have lived here,* she thought. Marie was turning to leave when she heard the bells again. This time the sound was directly under her. She looked down and bent over to put her ear to the soft dirt. There it was again, crystal clear below her.

She stood up immediately, backing away in fear. *How could the bells be coming from below?* she wondered. She turned around to head home but there was a shadow casting shade over her. There was the figure again, standing not two feet away. She could see the man very well. He stood there dirty from the ground, bells in hand. He was tall and slender, faceless and hairless. *How could this be?* She thought of any practical reason for how the man could have appeared in front of her.

She saw the stone in her peripheral vision and could see that the earth around it was not the same as it had been just seconds ago. The ground was torn up, and the grass around was pulled from the dirt. A small hole could be seen just in front of the stone.

Marie couldn't move. Her hands were frozen to her side holding her dress. The man stood still, unphased from all nature. All her previous encounters were when she was with someone, and the figures were always far enough away she wasn't too scared. But this was different. She was standing in the field defenseless with the man.

A hole opened in his face, and he said, "I'm still alive." It sent chills down Marie's spine. Then the man lunged towards her. She could not do anything to stop him. She fell to the ground and hit her head hard against the rough ground. There she lay alone in the field.

Chapter 3

Marie was able to make her way home after feeling like she had been stuck for hours in the field. *What happened?* she thought as she walked through the garden. *Who was that and what was he doing in the field? Why did the man attack her, then vanish from existence?* she pondered. Marie went to lie down in her room. She no longer wanted to read; she no longer wanted to do anything. She was just tired.

The next few weeks were normal, and she han't had an encounter with anyone since then. Her father's Easter spectacular went well, she heard. She couldn't recall most of the event. Her memory through these weeks had become spotty, only knowing what happened if people told her. One night she was in the kitchen alone, cutting up some vegetables. An urge took over her as she looked at the knife in front of the cutting board. Her eyes were glazed over and staring down.

Her father entered the room and said, "How do the carrots from the garden look? I tried the new soil that the market was selling."

No response.

"Hello, are you in there?" he said jokingly.

No response.

His tone changed when Marie turned around, knife still in hand. "Are you okay, peanut?"

Marie asked, "I am alive?"

"Of course you are, baby," he said, worried now. That was not Marie who said that.

Marie charged with the knife above her head. Her dad swerved to the side as the knife came charging down towards his chest. It missed his chest but sliced his right bicep. "What are you doing?" he shouted. Blood started to run down his fingers and a small pool was forming at his feet.

"Why am I alive?" Marie shouted, lunging again towards her father. He grabbed the knife hand and caught her. She was strong, way stronger than any girl her age should be. Marie's father could hold his own, though, and he disarmed her. She was panicking, swinging arms and legs in all directions. Her father called for help, restraining her as much as he could.

Marie woke up hours later at the church. She was confused, her hands bound together with rope. The pastor was talking with her father. He said an exorcism needed to happen as soon as possible. Marie was lost, unable to recall what happened. The last thing she remembered was looking up at the kitchen window and seeing the figure in the window's reflection. She couldn't hold back tears anymore.

Whimslet Village and Wolfseye Woods

SHAYLEE LUX

Whimslet Village is an extremely small and unheard-of village. Everyone loves everyone and helps each other whenever help can be served. However, three couples—Serafina and Nathaniel, Majorie and Clyde, and Ophelia and Phineas—are outcasts because they migrated there instead of being born in Whimslet Village. These couples decide to move out of the village. They start by entering into Wolfseye Woods, and the ground is covered with burnt orange and crisp red leaves falling from the surrounding trees. The couples look at the bark on the trees and at the sky, realizing that they don't know where the skinny, beautiful trees stop and the dark autumn sky begins. The air is crisp and chilly.

Nathaniel, Clyde, and Phineas discuss how weary these woods feel and just how much they are anticipating moving on past the woods. Meanwhile, Serafina,

Majorie, and Ophelia are overjoyed with the scenic route to their soon-to-be home. All three women feel safe and cozy in these woods, even after seeing bats, snakes, and foxes.

As the sun is glowing purple, pink, orange, and yellow, a castle-like mansion comes into view of the women. They convince their husbands to check it out and see if anyone is living there. Even though the men aren't excited about it, they eventually agree. As they walk into this castle, they realize nobody lives there and they can all live together there and still have room for children.

Ten years go by, and the men are constantly attempting to get their wives pregnant.

Serafina and Nathaniel both would rather not have children of their own. However, Nathaniel tells Clyde and Phineas that only Serafina has no interest in having a child because he would rather lie than let his ego be challenged. Clyde is constantly begging Majorie for a child. They are trying as often as possible, but anytime Majorie realizes she's pregnant, she gives herself an abortion. To Serafina and Ophelia, it is obvious that she had an abortion, but to all three husbands, it appears Majorie has miscarriages every year. Eventually, Clyde stops asking Marjorie to carry a baby. Ophelia and Phineas often have quiet arguments about her not caring about being a mother. Ophelia has sex with Phineas seven times, and each time, she has to ask if he has finished yet every couple minutes. After the seventh time of Phineas not being able to please Ophelia in bed, she refuses to have sex with him from that point forward.

The men start to assume that their wives refuse to have children because they're witches.

The women deny the ridiculous claim. However, the women are all very connected to nature, which only makes the men solidify their opinions. The men decide that their wives need to be put to death at the same time and that each husband is responsible for murdering his corresponding wife.

Nathaniel forms a dagger from the woods and stabs it once through Serafina's chest and once in her throat.

Clyde mixes poison with Majorie's coffee, and she feels the effects right away. She screams, and all the friendly animals surrounding the house are terrified and scurry away. After 40 minutes of terrible suffering and screaming, Majorie says, "You'll pay for this, Clyde, and so will Nathaniel and Phineas." Then she releases her final breath.

Phineas decides the best way to kill Ophelia is by putting her head under water while lighting her feet on fire. Every time she is able to bring her head up to get air, Phineas pushes her legs back so she is breathing in fire and smoke. After Phineas almost catches fire and jumps in the water, he pulls and holds Ophelia down in the water until she drowns.

Phineas, Nathaniel, and Clyde party in the castle until they get extremely drunk and decide to go tell off the village. Before they get to the village, they are attacked by bats, snakes, and foxes and die.

Just over three hundred years later, the castle has yet to be seen. However, there's the same number of people in Whimslet Village. Four friends want to go exploring in the woods: Samson, Ezra, Owen, and Silas. Samson is the mayor of the village, while Ezra, Owen, and Silas are all members of his advisory board. After making arrangements at their jobs and with their families, they start planning for a week full of adventure. Everyone thinks that the men will continue to have data on their phones while in the woods, but after walking seven feet into the woods, their phones are out of data. Even though their families start to worry, they decide that if they still have not contacted anyone by the end of the week, the village can send people into the woods to go find them.

The men walk around 20 feet before the sun starts to set. All four of them have been making small talk while making their first observations, but as the sun sets, they start to discuss how beautiful it is. Samson is the first to mention anything. "No, for real, though, the sunset is actually so pretty this evening," he says, taking a pause, "almost reminds me of how stunning Isabella is."

The other men know he is having an affair, but they usually discuss other things.

Ezra decides that one of them should respond to Samson and says, "So, how long have you been sleeping with your assistant?"

Owen and Silas look at each other, surprised. Neither one of them expected the conversation to continue. They look back to Samson as he responds to Ezra, "A couple of months now, but it's more than that, you know? Like, I actually feel that I might be in love with her. I just refuse to let Delilah find out."

Silas figures he should also chime in: "Do you think Delilah has any clue?" Right away, Samson laughs in a way that is evil and echoes throughout the forest.

"Are you kidding? She just thinks that I constantly work late and go in early. She's never even gone through my phone, but even if she did, I only let things that I could let my wife see. Everything else is on my burner phone," Samson tells the other men while they all are smiling.

The conversation goes on while each man tells the others about how they have been cheating on their wives as well. After walking 300 feet and insisting their wives have no clue about their affairs, a castle comes into view. Ezra is the first to see it: "Shit, did you guys know Wolfseye Woods has a castle?" They all agree that none of them has ever heard of a castle in the woods.

They all decide they should stay there for the night since the full moon is already in the sky.

As they walk into the castle, they see that a fire is already burning in the chimney, and the fridge is filled to the brim with various foods. They all question each other about how the fire and fridge are working. They decide someone must be living here and has gone out for something. They begin discussing the affairs they are having again, but before they can get even 2 minutes into the conversation, all the windows and doors start swinging rapidly. The men are scared. Owen even pees his pants, so they decide they should just head back to the village. But as they stand, the windows and doors all lock. Music starts playing from a record player in the middle of the kitchen table, where they are sitting. They all whip their heads to the record player and find there is no record to be seen. They all try to get up again. However, knives start flying. The men avoid most of the knives except for one. A knife slices open a vein on Simon's neck, and he dies instantly.

The other men are all screaming and trying to get up, and then they start hearing hysterical laughter followed by an angelic voice: "Did you really think you could have affairs without any consequences?"

The men start crying and fill up bowls that are placed at each seat. Another ghost starts to whistle for 3 minutes, takes a 3-minute break, and whistles for another 3 minutes.

After that, she screams, and everything in the kitchen starts falling, including a heart-shaped, blood-colored vase. It lands right in front of Owen and perfectly breaks down the middle. He looks down and sees a broken heart and picks it up. As he places his hand on the vase, it turns into a sculpture of his wife with her heart cut out. Then, without wasting any more time, black liquid starts seeping from the missing heart, then out of his eyes. His mouth is stitched together, but nobody can see any of the ghosts. As Owen brings his hand up to wipe off the black liquid bleeding from his eyes, he shoots up from his seat and through the roof.

Nothing happens for 7 minutes. Ezra and Silas both attempt to get up, but neither can move an inch. They are allowed to move their heads, so they start looking all around to try to spot anything. They feel something wet dropping onto their heads, so they turn their heads towards the ceiling and see Owen on the ceiling, dropping blood while burning into flames. After 7 seconds, he disappears.

All of a sudden, Silas can get up, so he stands up and starts to run faster than ever before.

He soon realizes that he is not able to dictate where he runs to. The ghosts give him a shot of a dark, red liquid. He faints but wakes up after 7 seconds. He looks around, and his eyes land on Ezra. Silas's eyes darken as he is running straight towards Ezra against his will. The second Ezra is less than a foot away, Silas opens his mouth. Ezra is now sweating as he sees teeth from Samson grow downwards into very sharp points. Silas bites into Ezra and refuses to stop until he drains Ezra of every ounce of blood.

Silas licks his lips and then starts running throughout the castle against his will.

He stops as he takes a breath and stops in front of a curtain. He is unable to move for 7 seconds, and then the curtains fly off. He closes his eyes, realizing the sun is coming up. The ghosts all begin to congratulate each other on successfully serving justice. After some laughter, Silas catches fire and turns into ashes without the fire spreading anywhere else.

Meanwhile, back in the village, the men and women in power are holding meetings to discuss when they should send someone into Wolfseye Woods to find Samson, Ezra, Owen, and Silas. The women propose to send a group of people of all genders who specialize in nature and self-defense. The women also suggest figuring out an idea for communication and sending a large supply of medical equipment, food and water, and survival equipment. The men in these meetings consistently cut off the women who give great advice. Because there are more men in power than women, the men control the voting. The final vote is that the village will send the last four men—Paris, Lawrence, Zadock, and Ethan—to figure out what has happened.

The women continue to tell them that the men should take their suggestions, but the men refuse.

After preparing for three days, the men start their new adventure. They discuss the same things as the men before them did. The only difference is that Ethan is surprised that these men are all having affairs. "You guys are actually insane. I could never cheat on my lovely Isabelle. You all took a vow when you married them. What is wrong with you all? Seriously," Ethan says about halfway to the castle.

Seven minutes later, after the men have been mocking Ethan, they arrive at the castle.

Paris, Lawrence, and Zadock decide they should stay there for the night since it looks abandoned. Ethan argues, "Guys, I think that this is not the most secure option. There could be creatures or other inhabitants in there." After losing the debate, they force Ethan to come inside with them.

After getting settled in the castle and joining each other in front of the fireplace, they begin to complain about the women in power in the village. Lawrence is the first to speak: "Can we take a minute to discuss the women in our council? Because, like, they are actually insane for thinking that we would need backup and survival supplies. Not to mention, their views on most matters are actually crazy."

"No, for real, Helen and Delilah are so crazy with their ideals. They actually believe that being gay is not a choice," says Paris.

"Guys, you are actually cruel to them, and their ideas lowkey make sense. Why does it matter who you marry? And Lawrence, why should we say no to survival equipment? Like, even if we never use it, it might be nice just in case we encounter a bear or a poisonous plant or something," Ethan says as the others all get angry with him.

"Ethan, you have so much to learn. You have only been in power for three months. Not only do they support the LGBTQIA community and suggest that we bring survival equipment, but they both are pro-choice. Come on, man, they are clearly trying to kill babies. How can you not see that?" Zadock angrily snaps.

"How is being pro-choice wanting to murder babies? Have you ever done your research and talked about it with them? Have you ever listened to what they discuss? The answer is no, because all you ever do is try to make your ego bigger. Well, I hate to break it to your sensitive soul, but it is literally impossible to make your ego bigger," Ethan says as they start to hear applause. The men all look around but find nothing visible.

All of a sudden, the fire goes out, and torches around the castle light. Then some loud, angelic voices start talking in unison: "Ethan, you truly are an amazing man, and we wish you nothing but the best of luck in the world." The voice pauses and then becomes angry. "However, the others, you all are cruel, and we would like to show some justice. Ethan, your justice will be served first. We grant you permission to leave the woods without any harm done to you, and if you try to rescue these horrible men, you will join their punishment." Ethan leaves and begins his journey back to the village. The ghosts start speaking in unison again: "Time for your punishments." The ghosts laugh, but they are tired of killing men, even when they deserve it, so they make these killings short. Afterward they start the fireplace again and throw all the men into the fire. Unfortunately, Zadock walks out of the fire and escapes the ghosts. He makes it to the village and touches every man who has ever agreed with him. As he touches these men, they are zapped by lightning.

The Wandering Day

EDWIN MULLER

It was a perfect day. One of those days you could've thought you were in a movie, the sun shining so bright it just makes you want to smile. My friend Carter and I had just gotten done with school. Approaching 3 pm we decided to head back to my house to play some basketball. As we were walking, Carter asked what my house looked like, having never been before. I explained to him that it was quite old but was very big! He asked if I had snacks at my house, and I replied, "Yes of course." We were both 17, growing boys who needed snacks every 3 minutes to survive.

As we approached my house after walking nine blocks, Carter and I were greeted by my dog Banshee. With Banshee jumping all over us, we struggled to get into the house but finally managed to sneak in. My mom approached us with freshly baked cookies. I had never seen her this happy. It seemed to be a special day for her, a day that reminded her of her father, otherwise known as my grandpa. Why was she happy, though? The memory of an open casket or a deceased human being doesn't usually bring happiness and smiles. I wanted to ask, "Why are you happy?" but my friend and I just took three cookies each and smiled and said, "Thank you."

After talking with my mother, Carter and I decided to go to the living room to watch tv. I set my school bag down and Carter put his right beside mine. We set down our cookies on the trays beside each end of the couch. Sitting on the couch, I realized the remote for the tv wasn't in view. I got up and looked under the couch. Nothing. Only a small French fry left from yesterday's dinner. I again got back up and decided to look through the couch covers and pillows, having my friend move. Nothing. Not even a single French fry was in sight.

I realized I had the same tv up in my room and it used the same type of remote. So, I headed for my room. I told my friend, "Stay in the living room while I go get the remote from my room." Walking alone, I started for the stairs. As I hit every stair, the world around me seemed to get darker and darker. Was it just because of the light fixtures in my house? The upstairs of the house barely had any windows at all. It practically felt like a basement. I approached my room taking a sharp left turn, having to turn on a light on because of how dark it was. Looking for the remote, I realized it was quite cold. Cold enough to give me goosebumps.

Luckily I had a heater, so I quickly turned it on and then kept looking for the remote. Finally finding the remote, I headed back down the stairs. Approaching the bottom, I turned right to find my friend not in the living room anymore. Not only did I not see my friend, but it was now dark outside. Confused but having completed the mission of finding the remote, I pressed the ON button to see if the tv would work with a different remote. Nothing. Complete silence. I yelled "Mom," and the only things that responded were echoes. I walked. And walked and walked to see if anyone was home. No one. Not even my dog barked as I yelled, "Is anyone here? … Banshee?" Now totally concerned I ran back up all the way to my room to find myself sleeping. Sleeping so silently with not even a breath to hear. Not even a single movement or gesture. Nothing.

I heard a faint noise downstairs! Something! So, I ran all the way back down to the first floor to find someone sitting on the couch. Thinking it was Carter, I said, "What took you so long?" Only it wasn't Carter. It was an elderly gray-haired man. I stared in astonishment. The gray-haired man got up from the couch, looked deep in my eyes, and pointed at me with his crinkly finger, saying, "What took you so long?"

The Emerald Eyes

BRI NARICK

I felt it again, only this time, it was stronger than the last. The concaving into my chest.

Not sharp, no. Dull. A heavy object, pressing into me as if it were trying to become one with me, so heavy that oxygen failed to reach my lungs. I was on my back. The ground was moist and cold. The smell of Mother Earth penetrated both my nostrils. I felt harsh and sudden bursts of wind that travelled down my entire body, leaving a trail of goosebumps behind. Frantically looking around, I was desperate to see what had caused the gusts of wind. My vision was cloudy. Whether it was the fog that engulfs the ground or the lack of oxygen in my body, I couldn't make anything out of the blur.

But then I saw it.

The choking of my breath slowed as I began to feel the pressure lift ever so slightly off my chest, a sign of mercy. I saw it. Out of the very corner of my tainted vision, I saw the large black figure lurk towards me.

I smelt it.

I smelt its breath, a hot tangy stench of death. Straight from the pits of hell. I felt its heavy pants, similar to the gusts of wind, but this time: warm. I smelt its cloak, that of thick, black, interweaving shag.

It cocked its head. My vision, still blurry, could not make out whether the glowing emerald orb in front of me was a god-gifted diamond or Satan's snakish eye. It entranced me, this circular light.

I felt the oxygen caress my lungs once more. It tasted like life. I lurched to take a breath.

I awoke, sitting up in my childhood bedroom, gasping for air in a throw-up pink room. The sun was beaming through my window, trying to blind me, and I rubbed my temples with my eyes closed shut, having realized I just had the same nightmare as the previous nights before.

I shifted out of bed, putting on the pink slippers that match the rest of the obnoxiously pink room, to pull my curtains shut. I resorted to going downstairs in my pajamas to escape the land of unicorns and a bigger headache from the pink.

I headed out the door and down the stairs, entering the kitchen where coffee was already freshly brewed. Before entering the doorway, I glimpsed my mother's hot pink Juicy Couture robe—can you tell she's got a thing?—before entering the kitchen. "Good morning sweet pea!" my mother said too cheerily for 7:08 in the morning. "Morning, momma," I said, smiling as much as I could at 7:09 in the morning. My vision was still cloudy from sleep.

"How'd you sleep last night?" she asked.

"Alright. I slept alright," I replied.

"You sure, hon? You know I could always have the movers switch out your princess twin XL with your queen-sized—"

"No," I said, cutting her off. I said it much too firmly. "I'm good … I don't want that bed in the house," I said more soothingly, trying to cover up the fact I had snapped.

"Of course, hon. I understand," my mother replied somberly. "Coffee's brewed in the pot over there," she said, gesturing to the bedazzled pink coffee pot.

"Thanks," I said, as my mother was already halfway through the kitchen doorway.

Now alone in the kitchen, I felt the guilt lurch into my stomach as I leaned against the countertop. I let my head swing down low, exhaling. It's not easy going through a divorce and moving back in with your parents at 26.

I lifted my head, eyeing the shimmering pot of Barbie coffee, and slumped over to pour myself a cup. I brought it to the table, sitting with the mug right under my nose. I began to recall the dream I had last night.

The air, my lungs, the smells, everything.

I had been having the same dream every night since I moved back into my childhood home in Weeting, England. Maybe there was something in American air that gave you the right to have different dreams every night, but here, it's been the same. I closed my eyes to make out the details. What I saw, what I felt. The whole dream felt so close yet so far away that I struggled to make anything out.

I gave up, opening my eyes. I took a sip of black coffee that helped ground me back to earth and decided that it would be best to get some fresh air and walk Teddy (my very tiny, scruffy, old childhood dog) around the neighborhood. Maybe a walk would help distract me from a mid-20s crisis and a stupid dream.

I changed into leggings and a rain jacket with boots, put a lead on Teddy, and shouted goodbye to Momma before stepping outside. The air was crisp and cold, nipping at my pale cheeks and turning them pink. I gave up on trying to escape the color. Petrichor danced around me, allowing me to fully appreciate the dew drops on spiderwebs that had taken hold outside of the house I grew up in.

"C'mon," I said quietly to Teddy, gently nudging at his lead.

As we began to stroll down my street, I pulled the hood of my rain jacket over my head, attempting to shield my identity from nosy neighbors who had decided that my mother's daughter's divorce was the newest hot gossip in town.

I kept a steady stroll, with Teddy gleefully leading us both. For an old chap, he really was a bundle of energy. I headed down Victor Charles Close, towards the church of Saint Mary's, where the remnants of Weeting Castle reside. Teddy and I kept a consistent pace, and I began to hear his happy panting. I imagined that every step I took was a step further from my past. A comforting thought, when my only worry in life at the moment was making sure Teddy didn't wee himself.

The church and castle gradually appeared as we passed small parks with children and corner stores selling fish and chips rolled in the Sunday paper. The smell of cod and vinegar could have made anyone's head turn, but the determination Teddy and I had was strong. We wanted to visit the castle

We came to a passing where we finally reached the grounds of the church and castle.

Teddy guided us over and through the graveyard that led to the ruins. We passed headstone after headstone, each one as different as fingerprints. Teddy stopped to wee on a headstone with the name "David Butler." It had no description or what he meant to people, but the name David gave me a bitter taste in my mouth after having been married to a David for 5 years. Teddy could wee all he wanted on the headstone for all I cared.

Reaching the end of the graveyard, we passed through rusty gates into the castle ruin's habitat. I stopped, and Teddy did too. For a moment it felt like we were both taking in the sight of flint and stone melding into one to form an architecture that looked like one only God could create. I lifted my head, trying to swallow the sight in front of me fully. It was so breathtaking that I choked on it. I rested my gaze down on Teddy, whose brown fur was ruffled by the wind. He looked up at me, and suddenly his panting stopped. His ears spiked up and made a full 180-degree turn toward the castle ruins. He turned back to me, jolting his body between my feet, whimpering and shivering.

"What's wrong?" I asked him as if he could understand me. I scooped up the tiny dog in my hands and held him close to my chest, shifting him slightly under the opening of my raincoat, a small attempt to stop his shivering. I could feel his tiny heart against my hand. It beat so fast it resembled a vibration.

As strange as it was, I wanted to keep moving forward. I didn't know if it was my reluctance to go back home and be reminded of my failure or an underlying desire to figure out why I felt so drawn to the place that kept me there. I looked back down at Teddy, whose heartbeat was still racing, and I looked forward toward the ruins.

I kept walking.

Entering the grounds of the castle, I kept Teddy close to my chest and continued with a confident stride. Something about the aura intrigued me. It was a magnetic pull. Calling my name.

And I had to answer.

I passed through the first hollowed-out entrance of what once was a room. The ruins were so dismembered that there were no ceilings whatsoever. I looked up to see the grey musk-absorbed sky and smiled. A wave of calmness washed over me.

I lowered my gaze back down, peering through the archway of what was left of the room.

I could see the pathway that led to the forest behind the castle grounds, the wall of trees resembling a horizon.

And that's when I saw it

A flash of black bolted into the forest. It was so fast that if I had blinked at the wrong time, I would've missed it. I froze, feeling a chill that ate away at any calmness I may have felt. But even after hearing every part inside me telling me to turn back, I slowly set Teddy, who was still whimpering against my chest, down on the ground. Before I took one step forward, Teddy darted back in the opposite direction from the forest. He ran so fast I had no time to grasp the lead properly. He ran and didn't look back.

I didn't move for a moment. My instinct would've been to go after Teddy, but something paralyzed me. My eyes were still fixed on the forest ahead of me, and before I could do anything to stop it, I began to walk forward.

As I walked, each foot began to feel less and less like my own. It was as if my legs were stuffed with cotton and tied to strings that someone above me was controlling, a puppet. Consciousness was no longer a privilege I had. I continued. Slowly, I realized that the feeling in my fingers, then my hands, then my forearms had disappeared. One after the next.

I was nearing the edge of the forest. Still being puppeteered by something much greater than me, I allowed this feeling to take over. The numbing of my body had been replaced with a feeling of floating, drifting. I let it take me. I wanted it to take me.

I finally entered the forest.

Whatever was controlling me had me set foot into lush forestry. I continued to intentionally walk with a strong sense of direction. I was not in control, but everything felt familiar. The smell was petrichor, but stronger than before. Mossy trees and shrubs stood so tall they blanketed the sky and any vision forward. I heard the faintest whisper, a hymn of h's and s's. I reached a small clearing. An oak tree in the middle, so big you'd think it was mother nature's Big Ben. I stopped in the middle of the clearing, only a couple of feet away from the tree.

I suddenly felt the bones in my body again. I lifted my hand, moving my fingers and trying to make out what had just happened.

A woman emerged from behind the tree. She was wearing a cloak so dark I could not make out any feature except for her bright green eyes. She turned to face me, staggering. I noticed she looked frail. Her face was pale and aged, her hair as grey as the sky had been, and her limping suggested she may have suffered an injury.

"Well," she said, inching closer to me, the emeralds in her face scanning down my body, "it's been a while since I've seen anyone around these parts of the forest."

"I'm sorry," I replied hesitantly. "I'm really not sure how I got here. I was walking my dog—oh, yes! My dog, he's run off and I really should be looking after him—" I was cut off before I could even turn around. My body had suddenly grown numb again, paralyzed. As I floated in the air, my body turned, facing the woman, and I noticed her outstretched hand. Her once wrinkly and uneven hand looked much smoother despite the awkward position of her fingers. Her posture and walking had improved too.

"You," I said through gritted teeth. I struggled to move my lips. "What's happening to me? Who are you? What do you want?"

"Shhhhh …" the woman hissed, "you'll ruin the fun part." She leaned forward, her sagging face now inches from mine. I winced, closing my eyes and pressing my mouth shut. I heard her inhale, slowly. Not a gentle inhale, a choking inhale, as if she was trying to gasp for air. I opened my eyes and immediately noticed that the once sagging and wrinkly face in front of me had filled with collagen and youth. A foggy mist traveled from my body into her mouth, as if she was sucking the life out of me. And it did not take long to realize what she was.

"Stop," I whimpered, the sound of my voice bouncing back to me as if my words were coming from another person. "Please, I'm begging you." She continued without flinching at my words. I felt my jaw tightening, making it harder for me to speak. I was dying. She was eating my insides. I was dying.

While still in the air, I began to feel a horrific sensation in my feet as if an animal was gnawing at the bones.

I managed to dart my eyes down, trying to navigate the pain. I witnessed my feet shriveling up like a deflated balloon, curving upwards. I screamed. I screamed with as much as there was left of me. I refused to accept this fate. My eyes darted around, trying to find something, anything.

Then I saw it.

A flash of dark darting through the trees just yards away. "Help—", I croaked. I couldn't scream anymore. Either this woman had a hold on my throat or my esophagus had already shriveled up. In the blink of an eye, a beast as large as a full-grown lion appeared behind the woman. It was so swift, but the image of its thick black fur ingrained itself in my mind. Its paws were enormous. Its claws were onyx black, as sharp as razor blades. Its ears twisted and turned as if it was trying to absorb every sound around it. Its nose, twitching. And its mouth, baring teeth so white, I almost winced. Saliva dripped down the sides of its mouth, landing like thick raindrops on the ground. But it took not a moment longer to notice a singular green eye sitting in the middle of its head.

The woman was still focused on me, vacuuming every last drop of life I had left. But without hesitation, the beast leapt onto the woman, digging its claws into her shoulder and sinking its pearlescent teeth into her neck. I heard the low growling of the beast and the screams from the woman. Her grasp released me instantly, and I dropped to the ground. Everything went dark.

I was on my back. The ground was moist and cold. I recognized this feeling. The smell of Mother Earth penetrated both my nostrils. I felt harsh and sudden bursts of wind travel down my entire body, leaving a trail of goosebumps behind. Frantically looking around, I was desperate to see what had caused the gusts of wind. My vision was cloudy. Whether it was the fog that engulfed the ground or the lack of oxygen in my body, I couldn't make anything out of the blur.

But then I saw it, something I thought I had seen only in my dreams.

The emerald, the eye. My attempt to focus on it strengthened. And it took not a moment longer to realize that there wasn't just one eye—

There were two.

The Dreamer

TESSA PEDERSEN

Darla Lewis was nine years old when she had the first dream. She had always had an affinity for the ocean and all its creatures, so it was no surprise that she would often dream about it. The dream started off out of the ordinary because instead of swimming through the ocean with imagined fins, she was at a marine park swimming in a large tank. She looked up at the surface of the water and saw a blonde woman with her hair in a ponytail waving to an audience of people in the short distance.

Darla's perspective changed and she realized that she was now in the body of the trainer. She gleefully kept waving before blowing her whistle to get the show started. An orca breached the water and bobbed its head up and down in the water before doing a spin. The audience cheered loudly, but Darla suddenly got a strange feeling in the pit of her stomach. In a flash she felt herself thrown deep into the water and away from her platform. She screamed for help as onlookers sat shocked in their seats. As she thrashed around in the water, trying to get to the surface, the orca caught her ankle in its mouth and pulled her down further.

A year later her dream came true. A trainer was killed at SeaWorld.

Six years after that, a now sixteen-year-old Darla had learned how to cope with her macabre dreams. They were rarer now than when she was a kid, and she was grateful for it. But lately the dreams had been becoming more and more frequent. They were vaguer than her normal dreams, and she did not know what to do. The dreams always started with her running blindly through a forest in the middle of the night, walking into a small cabin, and then running out of it.

She had never been the real-life victim of her dreams before. It had always been some unknown person in another state she learned about by watching the news. Darla had spent years trying to figure out the rhyme and reason behind her dreams, but she never could. The dreams always withheld the crucial details she needed to pinpoint the victim's identities, but that did not stop her from trying to figure it out to warn them. Now that it was herself that she must protect she was at a loss.

Another year passed and the only dream she had was the dream of herself in the woods and of that strange cabin. The dream would vary in length and in clarity, but the conclusion was always the same. On her seventeenth birthday she decided she had had enough. She was going to see it through if it killed her.

Darla waited until her father had gone to sleep before she tip-toed out of the house and made her way to the cemetery on the outskirts of town. She made a stop by her mother's grave to drop off a red poppy and to whisper a prayer to her. Darla wished that if the night ended in her death like all her other dreams seemed to she and her mother would be reunited again. She would have traded anything to see her again. After all, it was only after her mother had died that the dreams started anyways. She had always sort of wondered if that was why she had them in the first place, her brain telling her things about other people's deaths because she was too young to understand her mother's.

Once she was done in the cemetery, Darla quickly walked into the woods surrounding the sea of headstones. She got a creepy feeling that something or someone was watching her, so she walked faster and faster until she was running. She kept going and going, the trees around her becoming eerily familiar until her surroundings perfectly aligned with what she had been seeing in her dreams for over a year. Darla ran until her lungs burned and she tripped, falling to her knees. When she was able to calm down and get up, a cottage filled with warm light appeared before her. Holding onto her pocketknife tightly, she knocked on the door.

She waited with her heart pounding in her chest and in her ears before the door was opened by one of the largest men she had ever seen. He was young and dressed warmly in a flannel shirt and a brown jacket. Despite his size, she was not scared of him because the way he carried himself made it obvious he was a gentle soul. His shoulders sagged and he kept his arms close to his body to appear smaller. Even though it was well past midnight and she suspected he rarely had company, his expression remained neutral, like he was expecting her.

He explained to her that he too suffered from strange, seemingly prophetic dreams. His solution was to hole himself up in his little cabin and to research the people he dreamed about too, with the same luck as Darla. He told her that his name was John and that in his dreams she was being followed by something when she was chased in the woods. It looked like a sort of shadow, but it didn't move the way that a shadow typically did. When Darla asked him when the dreams started, he told her that it was after his elder brother died when he was in college. That's when everything clicked.

The dreams weren't happening by chance. The shadow in the woods wasn't a shadow at all, but a ghost. The ghost of her mother. Somehow the ghosts of their loved ones were able to send them dreams as some sort of communication. She thought maybe they were closer to the veil of death and could see it in others. They wanted to stop what happened to them and to save others. It just wasn't working too well. As she explained her findings to John, more and more made sense. Except for why she kept dreaming of herself. But John could fill in that dot for her.

He told her that he bet her mother could see that she was going to die soon and wanted to protect her. While most people would probably swoon with fright, Darla was not so scared. She felt an odd sense of relief. She would not have to carry someone else's demise in her brain anymore, just her own. Darla thanked John for what information he was able to provide her, and then she left despite his protests.

Darla stumbled her way back through the pitch-black trees and found herself back at the cemetery. She lay down by her mother's grave and waited with anticipation, begging for it all to be over. She stayed there throughout the cold night, motionless, until John found her the next morning, icy to the touch and eyes wide open. Dead.

Overwhelmed

ARTHUR PETTIGREW

Foreword: Names of various characters are concealed or altered for the sake of protecting their privacy.

Eight years. Hard to believe it has been that long since I first fell into that gripping despair at Hastings College. I'd be more likely to believe it if it were only yesterday or several decades ago. For it feels both recent and ancient to me. Don't ask me how that works, because I don't know either. But 2016, back when I was staying in Weyer Hall, will be forever etched in my memory. Always poking and prodding at the edges of my psyche. Constantly reminding me of those past failings.

But I'm getting ahead of myself. For this telling, just call me Allen.

Starting off, my first year at Hastings College just seemed to have what many consider typical challenges with adapting to living on a campus. Feelings of homesickness, changing lifestyles, meeting new people. The same happened with my father when he was a student in Weyer Hall. And he assured me I would do fine.

I just wished the neighbors weren't noisy some nights. Made it difficult to sleep. Especially one guy, I'll call him Noisy Boy for this, who kept making all sorts of strange sounds … some sounded like gasps, others like a struggling breath. No matter how often I asked this neighbor or anyone else, none could or wanted to elaborate on what the noises were. Not that he was a bad person, though. Far from it. Rather polite, all things considered. But that didn't make the noises any less unnerving.

I suppose I shouldn't complain too much about how my first semester went, considering how it was only closer to the end of it that I felt any of the burnout. And it wasn't as if I were plagued by the pranks my dad had faced when he was in this dorm over forty years ago.

But it was when my second semester was in full swing that … things went from weird to uncanny. My schedule was set to be busier than in the previous semester, but I figured I could handle it, considering I got through my first semester well enough. But experiencing the schedule in practice was starkly different from how I figured it would work. And it was getting harder and harder to care for both myself and my work. I felt a constant drain on my stamina as I kept going from one task to the next without adequate rest, as if the life was being sucked out of me.

But that's not the uncanny part. After finally getting the chance to relax after one particularly hectic week, I noticed that the walls of my room were not the usual wood and plaster. Instead, they appeared like a white, scaly surface with black dots and occasional splashes of blue, red, and green. All of that moved along on a rippling, scaly surface, as if there were writhing muscle underneath. But just as soon as it appeared, it vanished. I really wasn't sure what to make of that until I talked with some friends about it. With their figuring I had to have been worn out and needed a break if I was seeing stuff like that.

So, one of these friends, whom I'll refer to as Weird Bro, decided to take me over to the bingo event going on at the time. See if a change in routine could snap me out of my funk. Suffice it to say, neither of us got bingo that whole event. But there was the chance to get a prize if someone danced well enough to impress the staff and audience. I don't know what came over me, but I felt a sudden surge of confidence as I took off my coat and got up on the stage, much to Weird Bro's worry. Once the music started playing, I was … in a trance.

I don't remember what sort of dance moves I was doing. All I perceived were the vague echoes of the music, a strange, primal energy that seemed to guide my rhythm to what felt natural. And whatever I was feeling, the others in the contest must have felt, as well, for they were following my lead while my fellow Weyer Hall Weirdos chanted my name.

Now, I know I have some sense of rhythm, but a dancer that got people to follow his lead? That's a first for me. I wasn't sure what I did to cause that, but I was definitely out of breath. Both from the exercise … and just freaking out internally on how the hell I did that. It's like I was possessed by something … or someone, but I didn't have the nerve to tell anyone that at the time. I mean, who'd have believed me?

The brief break from my worries did help for a few days. Yet such wasn't enough to prevent my grades from slipping, even requiring me to cut out some classes. And in addition to all that, I had a bizarre nightmare, one in which I felt a sudden crash before feeling as if I were being crushed by an impossibly immense weight. Waking up, I felt an ache in my bones unlike any I had felt before. Even some of my intense exercises never made me feel this sore and tired.

I decided to try relaxing in Weyer Hall's common area, to have a wider space in which to stretch so I could alleviate some of the pain. But then another friend of mine, who I'll call Silent Cat, snuck onto the scene without meaning to, giving me a terrible fright. I was wondering what he wanted from me. He said he wanted to return a card I had traded to him earlier because the van delivering the package alongside so many others had gotten into a crash. The driver died immediately afterwards.

But as soon as that information registered, so did my earlier nightmare. Having a nightmare that just so happens to align with how someone died? I was feeling very panicky then. Not sure what to think. And I needed to head back to my room to gather my thoughts. Hearing about someone dying in a manner like a nightmare I had while also dealing with a falling-apart class schedule? That was driving my anxiety through the roof. And my capacity to focus on my work in such a state only plummeted further.

I was terrified to tell my parents about what happened, for I had always feared they would rip into me for not doing well with my classes. But even as they assured me they were more worried for my health than my grades, I couldn't help but hear a nagging voice in the back of my head that was much too cynical about the situation. It was cold and spiteful towards any other conclusion I could think of, berating me for bringing up the matter to begin with. Afraid.

"You aren't worth the effort giving accommodations to." "You coward!" "Quit being a lazy bum!" "Shut the hell up and keep working!" These lines and many more kept bombarding my mind, taking on the forms of my loved ones to twist the knife in deeper. Clashing with what I was just told about focusing on my well-being. And then ... I heard thunder. And I thought I saw lightning flash outside my window. But looking at my weather app, there was no storm anywhere near the area. I really needed to get some sleep. Otherwise, I felt I was going to go completely and utterly mad.

I still recall how even the mild winds of the spring semester tore through my body, as if a freezing-cold serpent were stinging my bones with icy fangs. And how the warmer weather in the late spring did little to help.

To think I had made a promise back in the first semester not to end up like an acquaintance of mine. He had his own struggles to contend with at college, though he certainly found some relief in being with friends who shared his hobbies. And he surprised himself with what he was willing to say to me about how overwhelmed he felt. But, in the end, it wasn't enough to keep him from pulling out due to failing grades. It seems that history is intent on repeating itself, even as steps are taken to avoid it.

What sort of curse did I bring upon myself to be such a damned fool about the situation? To not contact my loved ones sooner, to not come up with a better schedule, or to not be more assertive in getting what I needed? Even if it was only a temporary withdrawal rather than a permanent one, it didn't need to get to this point.

And why is it only now that I finally have the courage to bring this story onto the page? To put this menacing memory into a readable form? It's not as if sharing this will suddenly lift away the pain and grief I faced back then. And the echoes of which I still feel now.

I don't really know for sure how much of a difference it'll make, but I felt the need to pen this before I lost my nerve. Before the location where it all began was demolished. A lot has happened there, both good and bad. I met some of the best friends I could ever have there and felt the worst I ever have from a soul-gnawing isolation.

At the very least, I hope to save one brick from there for myself.

Victorian

KOURTNIE RITTER

The driveway seemed as if it went on forever, twists and turns that no normal driveway would have. As the Miller's car approached their new home, though, Ellie started to understand why the driveway seemed so extra. A house like this deserved a driveway that went on like this. A house like this wanted to be hidden away from the outside world. A house, no, more like a castle, is what it seemed like. Something you would find in a fairytale. The house was a total of three stories. It was made mostly of brick with huge windows the sun shined down upon. On the side, it had what looked like a tower coming all the way to a point at the top, taller than the rest of the house. It made Ellie wonder how old this house truly was. It definitely wasn't as modern as their old house, but it almost seemed like it was built 100 years ago or most likely longer.

"When was this house built?" she asked her mom, who was sitting in the front seat.

"I think the 1800s, so pretty old," her mom replied.

"Luckily the storms cleared up before we got here. I was sure it was going to be raining hard this weekend," Ellie's dad said as they got out of the car, changing the subject. Right before Ellie could respond, she glanced up at the second-floor window on the tower. To her shock, right there in the window, she saw a person wearing a top hat. Ellie raised her hand to wave hello, assuming it was some worker or maybe the relator welcoming them to the home. Before she could, though, the man disappeared faster than he had appeared.

"Who are you waving at, sweetie?" her mom asked.

"There was someone up there," she said, feeling as if she's seen this strange man before.

"I'm sure there's no one up there. I mean the doors are locked," her dad said as he flashed the key in front of their eyes.

"You're probably right. It's been a long day. I probably just need some sleep," she agreed.

That night Ellie was getting ready for bed when she heard the water turn on from her ensuite bathroom. "What the—?" she said as she approached the bathroom, only to find the water hadn't been turned on at all. The mirrors had been fogged up as if someone just got out of the shower. As she approached the fogged-over mirror, three lines that almost looked like claw marks appeared. Ellie couldn't help but gasp at what was appearing right before her. Taken aback she darted out of the bathroom, making her way to her mom's room.

"Mom," she called out, only to be met with silence. "Hey, mom, I think something's wrong with my bathroom," Ellie called out as she went to turn the door of her mom's bedroom. As she slowly opened the door, a sudden cold chill struck her whole body making her feel as if she were stuck in the arctic.

"You need to leave," a devilish voice called out as a black charred hand reached out from inside the door.

Ellie did the only thing she could think of … scream.

The next morning Ellie decided she would stay in bed a little longer, trying to figure out exactly what happened last night. She had come to the conclusion that it must have all been a dream since the only thing she could remember was jolting awake in her bed. Ghosts didn't exist. Houses weren't haunted. There is always an explanation for everything.

"How did you sleep, honey?" her mom asked as she placed a plate in front of Ellie.

"I slept okay. Hey, did I come to your door last night?" Ellie asked as she peered out the window.

"No, not that I remember," her mom replied.

"Oh, okay, guess it was a dream," she said.

"Your dad must have jinxed it," her mom said.

"About?" Ellie asked, confused.

"The weather's been storming since about three in the morning," her mom replied pointing out the window.

How did I miss that? Ellie thought as she stared. Sure enough it was dark and gloomy. Rain hit the windows like someone was knocking on the window forcefully trying to break it. "Good thing we got things moved in," Ellie said, noticing how long it had been since her mom started talking.

"Yeah, I really wanted to plant in the garden you know ..." her mom went on, but Ellie stopped listening. She couldn't shake the feeling that all of this was connected somehow: the man in the window, the running water, the mirror, the burning devil man, and now the weather.

Something was going on here; she just couldn't see how it all fit.

A few days passed and nothing strange or unusual took place. It was as if the strange figure just needed that one time and that was good enough. Ellie wasn't complaining about it, but it just didn't make sense to her. So, she did the only thing she could think of, research. She had asked her mom if she knew anything about the house, which was an immediate dead end. So, she turned to the library. "Do you have anything on the house on Hinton Hill," she asked the elderly librarian.

The librarian's demeanor changed suddenly. "Why would you want to know anything about that house? It was condemned years ago," she said. At that moment the world stopped turning, and slowly one ... two ... three ... long claws latched onto the librarian's shoulder.

"Watch out," Ellie screamed.

"Sweetie, what's wrong? Are you okay?" the librarian asked as the burning man started to get taller and taller, stealing more of the light from the room.

"No, there … there's someone behind you," Ellie rambled, trying to wish the images away.

"Honey, where's your mom? Maybe she can help," the librarian said, more puzzled. Then instantly the man was gone, just like at the house.

"No, no, it's okay. Sorry, umm, it was just a joke. You said the house was condemned. How can that be?" Ellie asked, trying to push past whatever just happened.

"Well, it was shut down years ago after what happened to the last family," the librarian said. How could this be? There was no way the beautiful Victorian castle that Ellie and her family lived in could be the same house as the one the librarian was talking about now.

"What happened?" Ellie asked, figuring there was no going back now.

"Well, about fifty years ago a family lived there, mom, dad, a daughter about your age, pretty like you too. They were a great family, always so nice to people.

Only lived there about a month before the so-called accident." She paused to catch a breath.

"What accident?" Ellie asked impatiently.

"Well, one night, it was storming badly. Anyways the family had just lay down for the night when the father got up at random, decided he needed water or something. But instead it was as if he just went mad. He grabbed a bottle of gasoline from the garage and doused his wife and daughter with it, then the rest of the house. Lit his daughter up first. He wasn't thinking, though, because he burned with them. All their bodies charred up. The weirdest thing, though, the husband only had three fingers," the librarian finished.

"How did he lose them?" Ellie asked, wanting to know more.

"Not sure, but there's a rumor that the original owner of the house possessed him and chopped off his fingers," she told her.

"Why?" Ellie asked, digging for more.

"Well, he only had three. He was some sort of mad scientist obsessed with fire," the librarian said as if this was all just a tale that meant nothing. In truth it should be nothing more than a ghost story, but too many things aligned for it to just be nothing.

"Do you have a picture of the original owner? It's for a school project," she lied.

"Sure," the librarian said, reaching for a book below the counter. The librarian showed Ellie a picture of a big group of people in front of her house. She didn't need her to point out the original owner, though.

She knew right away the man holding the shovel with three fingers and a top hat was the same man she saw staring back at her the day they moved in.

Ellie ran home as fast as she could. After the librarian showed her the picture of the original owner, she showed her a picture of the family. It was like looking at a mirror copy of her family, down to the very hair. Ellie couldn't help but worry that what happened to that family could happen to them. Not to mention the librarian said the house was condemned, so how did they move in? How is it not burned to the ground? It should be.

"Mom, who sold us the house?" Ellie asked, bursting through the front door.

"Umm, I'm not sure. Your dad was the one who arranged the offer," she answered, lighting a nearby candle.

"Well, where's dad?" Ellie asked, dread growing in her stomach.

"Out in the garage," she said, focusing on the light from the candle.

Ellie made a dash for the garage. "Dad," she yelled out as she came bursting through the door. She was too late, though. "What … what are you doing?" she stumbled.

"It's okay, sweetie. It will be over soon," her dad whispered as blood dripped down from the stumps on his hands.

"No, no, no," Ellie whined, but it was too late. She could already smell the smoke.

"So that's the house. Isn't it just beautiful?" the realtor asked the family in front of him. Ellie couldn't help but notice the peculiar way he dressed, with a top hat and cane, and gloves that only came with three fingers.

Part of her felt like she had seen him before, almost as if this were déjà vu.

"Yes, I think we'll take it," Ellie's dad exclaimed.

"What happened to the last family?" Ellie couldn't help but ask.

"Oh, they just vanished," the realtor joked. Ellie couldn't help but make a peculiar face. "I'm just kidding," the realtor said.

"Well, it's beautiful, perfect for our little family," her dad said.

"Perfect. You are just going to love it here," the three-fingered man exclaimed.

Death by Rattlesnake

MAX VERTIN

Professor Davis was the band director for Hastings college and his office was in Fuhr Hall. He hated his job, and all his students despised him as well. The professor never showed any compassion towards his teaching, and his students pulled pranks on him all the time. The professor was cruel to all his students and gave them extra work just to spite them. The students were going to make sure Professor Davis suffered for this and went a little too far with one of the pranks. Three of the students—Sally, Edwin, and Brad—had a plan to get rid of Professor Davis. The three students killed Professor Davis by putting a rattlesnake under his desk. Professor Davis was bitten without realizing it; he died 20 minutes later while still in his office.

Sally woke up in the middle of the night and felt guilty for something, but she couldn't remember what for. Sally had graduated from college eight years ago and was living with her fiancé Derek now, and they were getting married in November. It was now July. Sally got out of bed and walked slowly to the bathroom. As she was walking to the bathroom, her surroundings were changing.

Sally's house was transforming into Fuhr Hall right before her eyes. At first Sally thought she was dreaming and tried to wake up but couldn't. She then saw an orb of light coming towards her and heard the voice of Professor Davis coming from the orb. Professor Davis said, "I have come back from the dead for revenge, and I will haunt this house until the day you die." Sally immediately felt guilty and said, "I'm sorry for getting you killed. I didn't want it to end this way." Professor Davis accepted her apology and asked, "Where are Edwin and Brad? Where do they live?" Sally told him all she knew, and the orb of light was gone. She walked to the bathroom and as she was washing her hands she was bitten by a rattlesnake. She was unable to move and died 20 minutes later on the bathroom floor.

Edward is now the current band director of the Hastings College band and shares the same office as Professor

Davis. Everyday Edwin is reminded of how he is guilty of murdering his former professor. Edwin is miserable as a professor and is disliked by his students even though he tries his best and puts compassion towards teaching. He always tried to be a good professor because Professor Davis never was. One day, while Edwin was teaching, a weird feeling came over him and he felt a presence he hadn't felt in a long time. Suddenly all his students were gone, and an orb of light appeared in front of him. Edwin then heard Professor Davis say, "I have come for my revenge and shall kill you." Then the room went back to normal. As Edwin continued teaching, all his students were looking at him like he was a crazy person. When class ended, Edwin went back to his office. He sat down at his desk and was bitten by a rattlesnake that was under the desk. The snake disappeared as he tried to leave his office to go find help. The door was locked, though. He tried to yell for help, but his voice was gone.

Twenty minutes went by, and Edwin died in the same office as Professor Davis.

Brad plays bass for a rock band called Broken Love, and his girlfriend Vanessa is the lead singer. His band has been all over the country, and he has met many different people. Brad never thought his musical talent could ever get him this far, but just by playing the bass he got into a well-known rock band and started dating the lead singer. One night, after band rehearsal, Brad went back to his dressing room to change into clean clothes. He saw a bright orb of light and was filled with fear. Professor Davis's voice filled the room: "I have come for revenge. Prepare to die." The orb of light disappeared instantly and the room filled with rattlesnakes. Brad was trapped. All the snakes bit him at once, and Brad was dead within minutes.

After professor Davis killed Brad, his revenge was complete and he was at peace.

Listen Close for Crying

CASPIAN WEEDEN

It was another quiet evening. The crickets were singing their nightly song, and the rain at the window pitter-pattered gently. The moon shone through the misty clouds, shedding light onto the quaint house below. The boys had already been put to bed, and both had fallen asleep quite swiftly, despite the active humidity in the house. The kind, smart wife and her smart, kind husband had settled in the basement to watch television. The technicolor screen and gentle buzzing of the static were enough to cause sleep to slowly curl the couple into its warm embrace.

As the wife began to drift to sleep, she sensed something in the corner of her vision, a shadow peering between the staircase and the wall above the railing. She jerked upward and glanced around, but there was nobody aside from her husband, who'd reclined in his soft, green chair. She sighed and allowed herself to be swept up in the television again. Her husband coughed and she tensed.

"Dear, are you quite alright?" he asked, speaking in a low voice to avoid waking the children. His voice was typically booming and echoed through the house.

"Yes, quite. I believe I'm just being a mother," she replied.

This was the phrase they used quite often—though referred to as "father" when it was her husband who'd faced these thoughts—when they were thinking too much about their sons. It meant they were alright, but their parental anxieties were high. It meant the other needed to be present in case something truly did happen, because the first may be unable to respond as quickly.

And so the husband nodded, reaching his warm hand out to his wife, who gratefully held it. She turned her attention to the television again, trying to force her mind to settle once more. *Jeopardy* was on, the host laughing as he questioned the contestants on their personal lives. She sighed, and her husband squeezed her hand again. The two were often befuddled by the clue, but occasionally one or the other would know an answer and would nearly shout it out. Upon such noise, the other would shush them, reminding each other of the toddlers asleep upstairs.

Tonight was off, though. Despite the usual air of love and restfulness, the woman was quite the opposite, restless. Something about that figure earlier. As she thought about it, the creature seemed to come into view again, this time at the bottom of the stairs. It was trying to say something, but she couldn't make it out. She turned to speak to her husband, but he had fallen asleep, and she figured it'd be best to let him rest. She whirled back to look for the figure, but again it had disappeared. Goosebumps pricked up along her arms and legs and she let out an involuntary shudder.

Then a secondary thought: what if the figure was after the boys? If that was the case, why was it down here? Was it trying to assess the guardians of the home, how much of a threat they were to it? Questions kept running through the mother's mind, each providing fewer answers. How long had this thing been in her home? Had it already seen or—worse—tried to take her babies? What if she fell asleep? Would the creature take advantage of the moment? She hated that she didn't know the intentions of the shadow in her home. Did her husband have any knowledge this place may be haunted when they bought it? What was she talking about? Hauntings, ghosts, they didn't exist. She was sleep deprived.

Thunder cracked, and she groaned. As if she wasn't tired enough, now a storm had rolled in. Then her stomach dropped. The boys had been sleeping so well. Four nights with no disturbance until the sun started to rise, and now it seemed they would be going back to square one. The woman reached over to awaken her husband but jumped back when she heard a voice clear as day in her ear.

"Check on the boys."

She felt like she had been punched in the heart.

"Dear, wake up," she exclaimed. "We need to check on them."

"What's going on—" The man was cut off by his wife grabbing his hand and tugging him out of his recliner.

She didn't say another word, dragging him up the stairs. As they approached the door to the children's bedroom, the couple heard a quiet cry. The mother quickly pushed the door open and nearly screamed at the sight before her: her poor baby boy stuck between the railings of his crib and the wall. He was completely still, and not a cry to be heard. She froze, and her husband quickly stepped in. He crossed the room in only a few steps and reached for his son. Before he could grab ahold of the child, his wife spoke up again, her throat shaking with fear.

"I'm not strong enough to pull the crib back."

He nodded and slid behind her to the side of the crib. She carefully pushed her hands between the wall and crib until she had her son's waist held the best she could. Her husband grabbed the base of the crib and pulled. It started to move agonizingly slowly, and the mother had to stifle a cry as she saw her baby's skin blemished with bruises from the crib. As soon as the bed was moved far enough back, she readjusted her grip and lifted her child out of the way. Her husband pushed the crib back against the wall and then approached her,

placing one hand on her waist and the other on the tod-
dler's chest.

"He's still breathing."

The static finally faded from the mother's ears, and
she realized someone was crying. She turned to the
other crib, where her youngest was standing with tears
streaming down his face, a look of fear bright in his baby
blues, gripping the bars that held him in. He was looking past her, and she whipped her head around to see
the specter in the hall. It didn't move, simply watching
the events unfold and dwindling in and out of view like
a mirage. She realized this was the same figure that had
been in the basement, the same thing that had most
likely warned her of her child's accident.

Her husband whispered then, "What the hell?"

The figure nodded before walking away and dis-
solving into the shadows on the wall. The woman
couldn't speak, simply standing still as she watched the
specter fall out of view.

The Legend of the Blackfoot Cabin Catacombs

LEVI WEST

Long ago, there were Indian reservations built across Colorado. Upon one such reservation, after all its inhabitants had migrated for some unseen purpose, a camp was built for teens to get away from the rest of the world. They knocked down the buildings and rebuilt cabins into the mountainside for living spaces for the coming youth. Each cabin was named after an Indian tribe to give tribute to the people of past ages who had sanctified the grounds before those of present, even if such tribes had never stepped foot on the land: from the Arapaho, to the Cheyenne, to the Apache, to the Navajo, to the Comanche, to the Ute, to the Lakota, to the Cherokee, and lastly, to the Blackfoot tribe. The Blackfoot were the last tribe to have left the reservation, except it was not on peaceful terms. Legend has it that they left something there. For what reason or intention is unknown, whether they were trying to curse the land or the curse was there before and the Blackfoot were trying to save the forest area. Nevertheless a presence remained.

One year, outside of the sessions of the camp, three boys came to explore the campground with some rebellious intent. They stopped by the Blackfoot cabin and heard a soft humming, an eerie choir of seemingly female voices, but it was difficult to tell exactly. They entered the cabin and looked around, trying to find the origin of the noise, but it seemed to be coming from underneath the cabin. They moved the rug and found a trap door on the floor of the cabin, which seemed to be where the choir voices came from. As soon as they passed the threshold to the stairs, the choir silenced, and the boys went down, thinking someone to be in need of help.

Once they got to the bottom of the stairs, they looked down each pathway, which seemed to be made of some sort of stone. The most headstrong boy decided they should split up to find the girl or girls from whence the voice came.

That first boy headed down the hallway to the left and stumbled upon a room filled with wood and bones, bows and arrows strewn throughout the room. He noticed that the catacombs had grown colder and then heard a subtle hum, like a native call, different from that feminine chorus from before, their voices resonating off the bones. He walked around the room to the back, where there seemed to be an altar with nought but a silver arrowhead and a black footprint against the stone. As he explored the space, the voices went from subtle to evident to aggressive to not even a choir at all. They became a ghastly chorus, sourceless voices screaming a language he did not understand.

The boy, terrified, stuck out his hand and grasped the arrowhead, which had a string around it to form a sort of amulet. When he touched the arrowhead, the wailing became deafening. The boy began to run, and run, run, run, he did. The screaming died down, but something else, some other sound, entered his ears. Bones. The clattering of bones. Clang, clip, cloppety clop they sounded, faster and faster, but the boy continued to run, run, run back down the hall to the trapdoor.

He made it to the staircase when the bones caught up with him for taking their arrowhead; he felt a blunt force to the back, and he fell to the floor, unable to move but still aware of what happened. Back came that haunted choir, and he looked around for what had hit him, but there was nothing but scattered bones all along the hall, with an eerie white glow from the marrow of each fracture. And he lay there still, paralyzed with fear, too afraid to dare open his eyes again, hoping one of his friends would come back to find him and get him out.

The second boy chose to head down the hallway to the right. He remained cautious but at peace, as he believed spiritual forces to be nothing more than children's tales. As he walked, his nose filled with the stench of rot, like something had been mutilated and sat in that catacomb for years. He began to feel warmer and warmer as he continued down the hallway, but when he reached down to touch the stone floor, it felt cold as ice. He found a room covered in blood from the floors to the walls, with white fire burning endlessly on a sanguine dark stone sanctum. He explored the room and found nothing of physical interest other than the ruins of what seemed to be an ancient spiritual place, but to what nature he was unsure.

He was not sure how long he was in that room, as his thoughts seemed to race, but he got more and more lost in his own mind the longer he was there. As he finally began to turn back, he noticed something that looked like snow falling from a murky ceiling. Was it snow? No, it felt like ash. Bright, blue ash. And it began to burn. He heard a whoosh, and the fire moved towards him with a frightening speed. The boy ran. And run, run, run he did, but still did the fire catch him. The flames licked at the boy's flesh and scarred his back, but this only made him quicker. He made it back to the staircase only to find it covered in crimson. Clothing fragments were scattered around the hall openings, along with claw marks along the walls and the faint smell of wet animal fur. He looked down and saw a vaguely glowing silver arrowhead ...

The third boy explored the middle pathway. Giggling to himself as he went along, he came across an old tapestry concealing a passageway underneath. Not believing anything to be awry, he entered the smaller space and continued to make his way down. As he went, there were torches on the wall with white flames, but they seemed to give off less and less light as he continued. At some point, the bleak gray flames disappeared, and all was dark. But then he heard it, the breathing. Not a usual breathing, but a deep, heavy, and ethereal breathing. He found himself unable to move, and he could feel his heartbeat all throughout his head. Then he saw it. That vague cursed silhouette from which the breathing came. It was huge, must have been 7 feet tall, covered in obsidian fur: sleek, black, and reflective other than a small spot on its forehead. The shape on its forehead was silver, but that had not scared him as much as its eyes, fierce azure eyes burning with a ghostly flame. The beast howled and darted towards the boy, and, as he braced for impact and closed his eyes, still unable to move, he felt the forceful gust of wind and then *something* hit him, but not, it seemed, physically. His willpower felt sapped as he felt his soul inside his own heart hurt, but he did not have time to consider what happened. He turned to run. And run, run, run he did.

He ran, but he ran stronger, faster than he once did. He took longer strides and felt power. Anger replaced fear, anger for the world, his friends, that damned wolf; he continued in malice towards the staircase. When he got to the staircase he snapped as he saw that same wolf on the ground, with bones scattered behind him. In a fit of rage, he did everything he could to kill that beast, to be truly free of whatever had just happened to him. All he saw was the fury of claws not his own, and the body of the wolf flying around the threshold of the catacombs, until it was mutilated beyond recognition. He then flung it down the bone-strewn cavern. And then he realized his vision had changed. It had turned blue. Bright azure blue. He looked down at the puddle of blood from his earlier fury and saw that same bleak-hearted beast he saw stare at him earlier, those same ghost flame eyes staring back at him as his own. He tried to leave, but something pushed him back, a certain silver object on the ground, pushing, pushing, pushing with emanating power condemning him to this dark stone prison, back into his prior catacomb …

After the second boy reached the scene, he witnessed the bloody massacre and noticed footprints, barefoot, human as far as he could tell, all black, that seemed to glow grey in an uncanny light. Panicked then he saw the silver arrowhead amulet on the ground. In a quick rush of adrenaline, he picked it up and looked down the other two hallways. In one, he saw bones, bones, bones as far as he could see, and the other was pitch black, except for two azure blue eyes. Then, the eyes moved. He heard the clappety clappety clap of paw prints on that dark stone floor and growling, growling, growling as they got close. The boy ran up the stairs and flung open the trapdoor to leave but he felt a cold whisp follow him out.

The feminine chorus returned, but not eerie like the last time the boy had heard such a sound. It sounded like freedom, and the boy turned around, again curious of its origin. Only this time it was not in a helpful nature, but that of survival. He turned around and round again to see the cabin, which had looked new and fresh when they arrived. Now it looked … dead. Abandoned. And then he felt the cold rush through him and out again.

Startled, he turned around to see what he had felt just a moment ago, but nothing was there except those same black pawprints from before. That, and the clouds glowed an azure blue against the black night sky, and the boy felt fear. Fear so terrible that it pushed him to the earth, for the clouds resembled the horrific silhouette of a wolf-like beast. He felt his heart pumping in his chest, for he had escaped those catacombs with a shell of a life, but at what cost? To be trapped in a prison? The flesh that he embodied turned to his greatest curse? What had he released from that stony prison?

He thought, thought, thought some more until he could think no more, simply standing there in that clearing on the side of the mountain, just a stone's throw away from that horrific tomb. Ever still, the chorus grew louder and louder, and without thinking, the boy snatched a nearby rock and began to slam his skull, hoping he could make the terror in him disappear, along with that accursed singing. Blood spattered along the ground, and the boy began to lose consciousness. At last he began to feel his old normal self again, feeling nothing adverse at all, which he had not felt since he escaped that damned cabin. The last thing he ever perceived was the utter halt of the chaotic feminine chorus to an almost deafening silence: suddenly, all at once, gone. And then he, too, was gone.

Let Me In

LILY WILD

I remember the first day I saw him. He was tall and had brown hair that shined red when the light hit it right and blue eyes that anyone could stare at for hours. He was mysterious, his hood always covering his ears, those ears always full of music. He was a boy nobody could understand, a boy nobody could leave alone. He was a boy who couldn't stand to be seen—but he stood high, attracting all eyes to him. His narrative was made up by conjoined stories that those who surrounded us told. Nobody knew him, but everybody thought they did. He was a star on the basketball court, the reason people went—a joy to observe. When his name was announced over the speaker, the crowd would explode all chanting "Reese." It all seemed perfect, so everyone believed his life was just that—perfect.

I never spoke to Reese in the beginning. I, as the rest did, sat back and observed the lanky boy from a distance. We didn't cross paths much, and when we did, it was simple—I watched while he ignored. We were two different people in this small school; there was no reason for us to meet. My joy came from taking pictures, reading, writing—I was simply a shadow on the wall and I was content. I took pictures of all the sports, publishing them to the most recent edition of our school newspaper. I spent my time in many places, the football field, the gym, the courses—I captured the moments people forgot about. I made the stories come to life. I took pride in what I did, even though I was an outsider compared to everyone's sports-frenzied minds.

The time I spent away from the computer lab and dark room was in the auditorium. It was quiet and dark. Nobody bothered me, and nobody knew I was there. That is, until he started coming in. At first, I stayed silent, watching from the dark row that hid my silhouette, quietly observing the actions Reese Conway made. He had the same routine everyday: walk into the dark, secluded room, double and triple check he was "alone," slowly open the small door under the stage, and disappear under the platform. At first, I didn't understand the purpose of his need for escape, until I smelled the faint aroma of tobacco being lit. He would stay there for fifteen minutes, sometimes twenty, then he would crawl out of that microdoor, dust himself off, and walk out in his new relaxed state. This became a routine. One I began to look forward to. It gave me comfort that my presence was unknown, comfort within the norm.

Then, it was over. After weeks of silent observing, his words destroyed the simple routine. Reese walked in, his hood up as usual, music blasting into his brain. When he entered, I got a chill—maybe my conscience knew he would break our silent bond. I sat there, watching as the door slowly closed behind his towering body, his eyes finding my tranquil body, his legs stretching toward me. I sat there, still as ever, hoping maybe he would turn and walk to his trap door. But no. His body kept moving towards me. My breath caught in my throat. I felt as if something was tightening around my windpipe, struggling for breath as he slowly approached me.

"Hey," he said, his raspy voice ringing in my ears.

And just like that, his hoarse voice released me from my panic, and I could breathe again. I didn't get nervous around people. I had passed the stage where I felt the need to be accepted, but I had been watching him, and apparently he had been watching me too.

"Hi," I said, my voice sounding weak.

"How often are you in here?" he asked.

"Everyday." My response didn't seem to satisfy him, but he nodded his head and walked down the slanted aisle to his hideout. Within two minutes, the faint smell of tobacco reached me. It was a scent I had become comfortable with, but that day was different. The scent my body usually begged for, one that made me feel comfort, made me sick that day.

After that day, I didn't talk to Reese again. We continued our silent game, he ignoring me while I watched him. Nothing changed. He would strut to his hideaway, light his cigarette, leave the butt, and walk out. I began to feel as if I shouldn't be there, as if I should stop showing up. Let him have his peace. So, I stopped showing up. I let him soak in the loneliness.

I began to miss the silent watch. I began to yearn for the faintest scent of tobacco that I got so accustomed to. And most of all, I noticed the absence of not seeing Reese every day. I no longer saw him in the hallways. I no longer heard his name ringing in my head as I walked down the hall. He was gone—or so I thought.

I decided to go back to the auditorium. I could no longer stand the confusion—where did this boy go? I returned to my row, the dark swallowing me, and I waited for him to open the door. But the door never opened. I sat there for an hour, waiting for Reese. And he never came. So, I left, letting his absence hang in the air.

After weeks of Reese's mysterious absence, I moved on. I stopped looking, I stopped thinking, and I lost the desire to ask where he went. Nobody else seemed to notice, so maybe it was just me. I began to spend the rest of my time in the computer lab. I would take pictures, go to class, eat lunch, and stay in the computer lab till I was forced to go home. I became comfortable in who I was and what I enjoyed again.

Then it came out. Reese was gone. He died under the stage of the auditorium. When he went down for his smoke break of the day, he got stuck and couldn't get out. The weeks that passed where he was missing, he was stuck under that stage. His body began to rot, the putrid scent saturating the air in the dark, empty-seated room, his eye sockets sinking in, making his structured face look aged and unwell. Reese Conway's perfect little life was over, and reality set in.

The basketball court was empty after Reese Conway took his last breath under the auditorium stage. There wasn't any more yelling or chanting, especially on the night they recognized his passing. Nobody looked for the tall, blue-eyed boy in the hallways anymore. He was simply forgotten within the student population, and the obsession was over—at least for most people.

When I entered that enclosed, dark, damp auditorium after he passed, I sat and wrote my papers, taking in the peace of being alone—fully alone. Then I began to hear faint noises. It sounded like music playing, but it was muddled—as if it were blasting through someone's headphones. I didn't recognize the song playing. It was too quiet to pick up any words or even a rhythm, but I know I heard it, and it was coming from the stage. All I could think was Reese. He was the only thing that came to my mind. I tried to ignore the faint notes, but they seemed to get louder, clearer, closer. I chose then that I was not going to let the game Reese and I played set my mind off. I packed my bag, and I trekked to the door, the music following me.

Louder and louder and louder. As soon as I pushed that door open, it stopped. I didn't return to the auditorium after this incident.

I roamed the halls when I couldn't write. I'd let my fingers trail the crevices of the off-white brick walls. The halls were short, making my laps go by faster and faster each round. I didn't think about much. My mind mostly just wondered about the most random things. Sometimes I would think about writing, sometimes I'd think about food, and sometimes I'd think about Reese. It wasn't often, but every now and then his name would cross my mind. I wanted to know why he needed his tobacco escape and why he always hid himself beneath a hood. There were so many unanswered questions, and they would stay that way forever—Reese Conway's story will forever be a mystery.

One day, I was thinking about Reese, about his shortened athletic career, his shortened life, how unfair this was all because he wanted to feel free in a different reality, when I heard a basketball bounce. My legs stopped moving forward, and my finger stopped tracing the broken wall. I heard a basketball bounce again, but when I looked around, there was nothing. I began walking again, and there were two more bounces—this time they were right behind me. I stopped. I listened. And I swear I heard someone breathe behind me. I turned and there was nothing. Nobody. I picked up my pace, quickly walking to get out of the athletic locker room hallway. And the bounce followed me, quicker.

Quicker. Quicker. I turned the corner, and the bouncing stopped. What is going on?

I stopped frequenting that hallway after that. Nobody mentioned anything about the sound of a ball bouncing or the faint music playing in the auditorium. I thought maybe I was losing my mind, but I wasn't going to test that theory and go back to those places. I kept to myself more and more, scared that if I went down the wrong hallway it would happen again. I was paranoid I would be chased by the bouncing ball or the muffled music. I was scared. Scared that Reese Conway would catch up to me. Scared that he found out I forced that small door shut.

Aphrodite

KIEFER ZABEL

Growing up in a small mountain town in Colorado came with some hard-to-believe stories. The Tommyknockers Curse was the most heart-stopping tale of them all. Miners believed that tommyknockers banged on the walls of a cave when a collapse or accident was imminent. Some believed the tommyknockers caused these accidents, either out of spite or as retribution. Such an accident happened to Watson Strong, who met an unfortunate fate because of who he loved.

The accident happened in 1943 in the mining town of Idaho Springs, a booming city that started the gold rush out west. In 1893 the Strong Family found gold in the Chicago Creek and started The Argo, a large gold mine. With Idaho Springs becoming a booming mountain town, Central City being only 5 miles away, it was the best place in the state to gamble and with the highest stakes. The Argo was producing 100 million dollars

per year, until it had to close due to a catastrophic acci-
dent. Watson Strong was the lead operating miner in
The Argo's main operating tunnel, the "New House
Tunnel," which was 4.2 miles long.

At the time, Watson Strong was 33 years old. He
had grown up in the wealthiest family in Idaho Springs,
but his childhood was less than ideal. His mother
passed away during childbirth, and his father was often
away running The Argo. Growing up in a wild, booming
mining town was challenging enough, but being raised
by multiple nannies and having no father figure to give
him moral direction had effects on the boy. He learned
that if you work hard and be bold, you could make a lot
of money in this community. This made Watson very
successful, becoming financially sound and building a
very nice physique, but he always desired attention to
fill the emotional void of his childhood.

Watson was a student athlete in high school but
was always an outcast since everyone knew he was
the rich kid and treated him differently. Everyone
was afraid to talk to Watson except the Radley Twins,
Timmy Radley and Elanor Radley. Timmy was very

closed off and let Ela do a lot of the talking, but Timmy was a savvy chess player. He was a silent assassin on the chess board, which was the only time he showed that he cared about anything. Ela was a solid tennis player but never had any exposure to showcase her skills since the high school didn't have a tennis team. Watson made sure they could enjoy these activities, which made the Radley Twins depend on Watson and he would do anything to stay with them. These three were inseparable, doing everything together once they met in high school. They all had after-school activities and would cheer each other on, study together, and push each other in the classrooms as well. Watson, though, always had his eyes on Ela. Both athletes, they would work out together often.

Watson had any option he wanted for college due to his money and pure athletic ability, but Ela and Timmy didn't have that luxury and only had the option of going to The Colorado School of Mines, which specialized in drilling and explosions. Watson wanted to attend Colorado University to play football, and the financial wealth of his family allowed him to offer a scholarship to a friend, but he had to decide between Timmy and Ela. Timmy was always his man, and he wanted him to be his best man when he got married, but Watson thought chess was just a good bar game that has its challenges. He didn't feel it would be worth bringing Timmy to CU. Watson picked Ela to go with him to CU, knowing she would have a real tennis team to join and being able to compete at the national level would be the best for her athletic career. The choice seemed obvious.

During sophomore year, Watson and Ela fell in love, while maintaining good relationships with Timmy as he was excelling in drilling. Watson and Ela planned to marry back in Idaho Springs, on Valentines Day, so their families could celebrate this coming together of love, but Ela fell ill during travel and was bedridden once they got to the Strong estate. Timmy started out to the estate for the wedding but stopped in Central City a few days early to gamble. He was having a difficult time being separated from his twin and having his best friend marry his sister, but he wanted to see them anyway and planned to attend the wedding. Since the wedding was postponed, Timmy decided to stay in Central City and gamble and drink more. While Ela rested, Watson went over to meet Timmy at the casino and could feel the jealousy and slight hatred from Timmy as the night progressed. But Watson was having fun, and Timmy was happy to have his old friend back. As the night came to a close, neither Timmy nor Watson was fit to ride a horse, so they stayed in the tavern. There was only one bed left, though, so they had to share. Watson was so happy that Timmy still gave him attention that he cuddled extra close to Timmy that night.

In the morning, as they rode to the Strong estate to see Ela, the vibes were high with their winnings (mostly Watson's). As they got to the house, they found the door ajar and the house cold. The air inside felt as cold as the night, making them wonder if Watson left the door open when he left the night before. He couldn't remember. As they went inside, they called out for Ela. With no response back, panic began to fill both Timmy and Watson. They searched the whole house, but neither were able to find Ela.

Once Ela went missing, both Timmy and Watson worked at The Argo and searched the mountains in hopes of finding her. Neither Timmy nor Watson wanted to sleep in the bed that Ela last slept in, so they shared the master bedroom. While Watson was the lead mining operator, Timmy was his second hand. They were usually together.

On February 25th, 1943, exactly 10 years after Ela disappeared, Watson and Timmy were blast mining in Aphrodite, a tunnel system that stemmed off New House, when they hit an aquifer, flooding the tight cave quickly. The aquifer was so big that a Boeing 747 could spin around 360 degrees in it and not touch a single rock in that cave. Watson and Timmy were killed, along with 76 other miners, and the flood washed out the entire east side of town and destroyed the Strong estate. As the flood waters receded from the Strong estate, a mystery was revealed. Ela's body was found underneath the Strong estate, which made townspeople wonder what really happened when Timmy and Watson came back to the bedridden Ela. Was she ever even sick? We will never know.

www.ingramcontent.com/pod-product-compliance
Lightning Source LLC
Chambersburg PA
CBHW070953180726
48291CB00004B/1271